DÉSIRÉE CONGO

CARAF Books
•

Caribbean and African Literature
Translated from French

Renée Larrier and Mildred Mortimer, *Editors*

DÉSIRÉE CONGO

a novel

ÉVELYNE TROUILLOT

TRANSLATED BY M. A. SALVODON

Afterword by Annette K. Joseph-Gabriel

UNIVERSITY OF VIRGINIA PRESS
Charlottesville and London

The University of Virginia Press is situated on the traditional lands of the Monacan Nation, and the Commonwealth of Virginia was and is home to many other Indigenous people. We pay our respect to all of them, past and present. We also honor the enslaved African and African American people who built the University of Virginia, and we recognize their descendants. We commit to fostering voices from these communities through our publications and to deepening our collective understanding of their histories and contributions.

Originally published in French as *Désirée Congo* by Éditions du CIDIHCA, Montréal, 2020, © Évelyne Trouillot

University of Virginia Press
This edition © 2024 by the Rector and Visitors of the University of Virginia
Translation © 2024 by M. A. Salvodon
All rights reserved
Printed in the United States of America on acid-free paper

First published 2024

9 8 7 6 5 4 3 2 1

LIBRARY OF CONGRESS CATALOGING-IN-PUBLICATION DATA

Names: Trouillot, Évelyne, author. | Salvodon, Marjorie, translator. | Joseph-Gabriel, Annette K., writer of afterword.
Title: Désirée Congo : a novel / Évelyne Trouillot ; translated by M. A. Salvodon ; afterword by Annette K. Joseph-Gabriel.
Other titles: Désirée Congo. English
Description: Charlottesville : University of Virginia Press, 2024. | Series: CARAF books: Caribbean and African literature translated from French | "Originally published in French as Désirée Congo by Éditions du CIDIHCA, Montréal, 2020." | Includes bibliographical references.
Identifiers: LCCN 2024010102 (print) | LCCN 2024010103 (ebook) | ISBN 9780813952116 (hardcover ; acid-free paper) | ISBN 9780813952123 (paperback) | ISBN 9780813952130 (ebook)
Subjects: lcsh: Haiti—History—Revolution, 1843—Fiction. | lcgft: Historical fiction. | Novels.
Classification: LCC PQ2680.R656 D4713 2024 (print) | LCC PQ2680.R656 (ebook) | DDC 843/.914—dc23/eng/20240315
LC record available at https://lccn.loc.gov/2024010102
LC ebook record available at https://lccn.loc.gov/2024010103

Cover art: Market Scene, Bouta, twentieth century. Oil on canvas. (Detroit Institute of Arts; gift of Roland Wiener in honor of his children, Alice Gerard and Charlotte Wiener, 1996.252)
Cover design: Cecilia Sorochin

To Pierre Buteau, the historian whose friendship and thinking have accompanied me throughout the writing of this novel.

A big thank-you to the strong and beautiful group of family and friends who reread the manuscript and who shared their comments and suggestions with me.

Thank you, too, to those who were willing to hear me talk about the novel and who showed interest. I take responsibility for any misreading of their ideas and interpretations.

The plunge into the chasm of the past is the condition and the source of freedom.

—Frantz Fanon, *Toward the African Revolution*

1804: The end of an epic. Haiti becomes independent after almost half a million Africans free themselves by force of arms.

1804: The racist European and American leaders watch in fear the sudden and unlikely emergence (despite the signs) of an independent Haiti, built on the ruins of the most profitable colony that Europe had known till then.

1804: It was a rupture ahead of its time, and I would even say (what blasphemy!), ahead of History as it had been experienced by the world. The consequences are as noble as they are turbulent.

—Michel-Rolph Trouillot, *Les racines historiques de l'État duvaliérien*

CONTENTS

Translator's Acknowledgments	xi
Translator's Note	xiii
PART ONE	3
PART TWO	77
Afterword	187
Bibliography	197

TRANSLATOR'S ACKNOWLEDGMENTS

In gratitude to all the people in my different communities who made it possible for me to do this work, I dedicate this translation to you. To Luce, Rose Marie, and Alice, whose wonderfully fierce and all-encompassing motherlove continues to nourish me. To my beloved grandmothers, Man Cia and Mè Ta, and grandfather, Papa Ton, whose sweet and resonant voices filled with admonitions and playful entreaties I can still hear so clearly. To Tante Emilie and Tonton Jacques, whose peals of exuberant laughter still resonate. To Maman Nelly and Papa Y, whose home in Musseau was a sanctuary where I first became terrified of *zandolit,* enamored with trees, and obsessed with dictionaries. To my extraordinary father, Jean Léon, for showing us how to live fully in every moment, for being a brilliant model of empowered perseverance, and for keeping the Haitian language and Haitian history alive in our hearts and minds. To Shay Youngblood, for being a force of nature, a member of my tribe, a fierce and beautiful writer, a generous, loving, and exuberant presence—even from afar. I love you forever. *May your spirit soar high and free.* To my family, both near and far, chosen and biological: for listening attentively, for drinking coffee, doing puzzles, and making art, for walking among trees from sunrise to sunset, for the early morning raucous laughter, for the phone calls and Zoom visits, for thinking with me about writing and translation, for sending me a steady stream of messages, books, and articles. Your love and encouragement from Altadena, Atlanta, Attleboro, Baltimore, Cambridge, Corseaux, Dakar, Dorchester, El Cerrito, Jamaica Plain, Léogâne, Lexington, North Miami, Montréal, Montreuil, New York City, Paris, Port-au-Prince, Portland, Roxbury, Somerville, Tepoztlán, and Woburn accompany me on all of my life's big, messy, and most memorable adventures. To Renée Larrier and Mildred Mortimer for their enthusiastic support. To the anonymous readers of the manuscript for your very insightful comments. To two very inspiring friends whose boundless generosity and keen intellect are gifts to the world and to me: Micheline Rice-Maximin, for teaching me to engage deeply with words, for three decades of puns, and for embodying *kimbe rèd, pa moli;* Sue Lanser, for her constant encouragement and meticulous reading of this translation. You are both models for living lives filled with kindness, wit, and integrity, while cultivating the seeds of friendship, solidarity, and community all over the world. To Évelyne Trouillot, for writing captivating historical narratives that evoke the fullness of the many people whose experiences are not easy to find in archives, and for bringing the force of Haitian history alive. *Mèsi anpil.*

To Haiti, our people, our country, our language—*Ayiti pap peri!*

TRANSLATOR'S NOTE

I've always understood the high stakes of the art of interpretation and translation. At best, a misinterpreted word causes mild confusion, at worst it causes misunderstandings that communicate an incorrect meaning and provide false information. Children of immigrants, like myself, who are raised speaking the languages spoken by their parents understand the risk and appreciate the gift of moving from one language to another. The traditional Haitian greeting in which one person says "Onè" (Honor) to which another person responds "Respè" (Respect) is a salutation based on mutual acknowledgment and appreciation. It is precisely this kind of exchange in literary translation that is informed by the ethics of honor and respect for words and the contexts in which those words are used.

The experience of translating *Désirée Congo* was one that required my full immersion in the multiple stories depicting varied groups of people who were living in the years leading up to the decisive Battle of Vertières in November 1803: the enslaved women, men, and children, the Creoles who were born on the island as well as the Africans who had been brought on ships—including the not-yet-born who traveled ensconced in their mother's wombs—the mixed-race children and adults, the maroons, and the planters. This multitude occasioned a wide range of racialized terms, which I do not capitalize. This decision universalizes all the racial categories as ones constructed within the plantation society context. The full humanity of the enslaved is most visible in their actions, in the stirring of their hearts for liberation, and in the strategic calculations of their minds—and not in the names that the enslavers imposed on the more than half a million women, children, and men brought to Saint Domingue in the eighteenth century alone. In diving deep into the vocabulary, sentence structure, and rhythm of the narrative, I encountered the unrelenting violence, persecution, and terror endured by the enslaved as well as their sparks of creativity, moments of collaboration, and dreams of revolution. In a novel that evokes a multitude of experiences, the singularity of each character informed my decisions: Which word best captures the sense of the experience evoked? How do I stress the nuance of a particular perspective? How do I best reflect the ambiguity of a complex interaction?

Traveling across a wide expanse of oceans, mountains, and centuries, I imagine my ancestors. Each word translated, a bridge. Each sentence, an ode.

DÉSIRÉE CONGO

PART ONE

The first time he saw her, she was skipping in the distance with open arms, which fluttered around her like multicolored wings. Zinga thought her body was covered with flowers or lit up by a rainbow shining for the sole purpose of circling her figure. He hadn't stopped looking for her since then, watching out for the slight hint of color that would precede her arrival. Several days went by before he saw her again. So despairing of never seeing her again that, despite his reticent and secretive nature, he forced himself to ask another African from the encampment about her. He tried to describe her, having seen only her movements and will-'o-the-wisp figure, elusive in broad daylight, beautiful and unattainable. The African exploded in a laugh that Zinga considered crude and ugly. With a scornful gesture of the hand, he said, "That's Désirée, the daughter of the negress Aza. Be careful, she can cast a spell on you." He didn't listen to this senseless chatter, not wanting to ask for details or for any more information. Her name. He knew her name, and for now he would be satisfied with that.

He approached her weeks later. She had already taken hold of his spirit, and his *bon anj* had already attached itself to the ample skirt that brushed against her calves. He had stopped half-hidden by the trunk and bushy leaves of the mango tree—not for fear of disturbing her dance. He could see that she couldn't care less about the glances cast by others. He remained quiet to better take in her movements. Was it really a dance? Was it maybe a game? She would spin around, bend forward, lower herself, then straighten up slowly, then begin skipping again, with her fingers slightly closed as if she were shaking the hand of an invisible friend.

The supple nature of her movements, their playfulness, fascinated him. Long afterward, he remained nailed to the spot, unable to turn his eyes away from her figure fading in the fog.

I'd like to stay here all the time, on the very top of the mountain, from up here I see everything, and no one sees me. And I can play unbothered, without having to meet Ma's eyes. She doesn't know that I can feel it when she's looking at me. The weight of her eyes on my back tells me all the things she wants to hide from me. In her eyes, I see her sadness and her anger. She doesn't know that at night, I hear footsteps pounding the hut's dirt floor, I hear grunts, and sometimes I hear the sound of slaps. I hear a harsh voice falling like a machete on a sugarcane stalk. Ma's eyes make me shudder. I snuggle in her arms without looking at her for too long. But her arms also communicate her anger. Sometimes they hug me so tightly it hurts. Ma Aza doesn't laugh often, and when I do, she always turns her head as if surprised by my expression of joy. It's as if she knew that my laughter is often merely a white lie—a fable, a tale, a veil. It's her courageous and generous smile that keeps me from falling. Her smile gives me some of her strength. Ma is strong. I've inherited my long and solid limbs from her. She says I really get them from my father—this father who remains back there, and whom I don't know.

My younger brother, Guillaume, tells me that fathers are sometimes useless, but I know that I would have loved this papa of mine whom I've never met.

Ma smiles. Me, I laugh. At times when I laugh, I feel Ma's lips on my face as if she were lending me her smile. Without it, I would never have learned to laugh. But I think the sadness of her eyes has become a part of me, I carry it also in mine.

All around Zinga, the mountains stood tall. In a few months, fog would surround them with its grayish envelope. This allowed him to lull himself into believing that he was still home: in the constant drizzle almost every month of the year in the extensive high plains where he was raised. Even during the hottest months, if it rained less often, it still rained. It would appear suddenly, cooling the air, and the ever-present humidity would rise. He never would have thought that he'd long for that heavy, humid air, but sometimes the longing to see those wide, open spaces would fill him with a pain that he would try to relieve in vain, with mouthfuls of hatred.

Even after these long eleven years, his body still experienced fleeting moments of nostalgia that clouded his vision. Sweat dripped down his sides, and the old scarf that he had wrapped around his neck was soaking wet. He would touch the ground in quick strides and feel the warm, dry earth work itself into his toes and enter his body, reminding him that he had been taken away from his world to be transported here.

Since arriving in the colony, he'd perfected the art of disguise, the ability to make himself invisible in order to better observe everyone else, those people who thought they could mold him to suit their purposes. He had yielded, but his back had hardened in order not to falter. He had learned to sniff out danger well before it materialized into men from the constabulary searching for new flesh to flog. His feet had learned to avoid the too rough stones and open paths to be able to weave through the thickest branches and merge with the flurry of leaves and wind. Sometimes he would tell himself that if he had acted with as much prudence on that deadly day long ago—if he had known that savage, armed men were lying in wait to sell them to the whites—he would have quickly returned home, where his mother and sisters were waiting for him. Or he would have joined his father, and together they'd have gone hunting before returning home. But when he'd come upon his friends Sinchi and Pauban along the way, he'd joined them on that fateful day. Back then, his mother called him "eldest son full of promise," and he still had the lightheartedness of someone whose eyes open onto a world that he thinks will always be his.

The sighs won't tell a different story from the one they had carved on his young gangly adolescent skin, on his torso that had been toned up by labor in the workhouses: the steady and arduous movement of the mill grinding, until he had had enough of watching himself become a mule, just like the others who operated the machines that peeled the bright red fruit flying all around them. Just like the four-legged mules that powered the grinding mill of this famous coffee that was making other people rich.

Even before reaching full adulthood, Zinga the African had rejected the name "Jean-Philippe" that the planter wanted to stick on him. He stopped for a moment amid the shrubs whose shiny and unseemly green leaves, somber and soft, attracted him in spite of himself. The mesmerizing scent of the white flowers, all bunched together like a bouquet, always awoke in him the desire to rediscover the tenderness of long ago. Images came to him—his mother laughing in silence—as if to contain the joy that filled her breast while her two arms opened to hold her children and keep them in her joy. How had she borne his absence? How had she survived his disappearance? Was she still alive or had they taken her too aboard one of their ships?

How could he know, since it has been so long since he had ended up in a world so foreign? Right in front of him, on that very distant day, he had seen Sinchi's blood shed and knew that his friend had died. He didn't know what happened to Pauban. Since having fled the workhouse and having escaped the long exhausting days, where every move he made gnawed at his dignity, where the blows threatened to make him forget the ritual markings on his father's face, he had tried to learn more. He had figured out who had come from his corner of the world, he had asked questions, dug through their memories, and felt their suffering rise again along with his own. Sometimes he would have preferred to forget everything. But he knew that it wasn't in the natural order of things and that this wound would always be a part of him. He had met many people, most of whom had arrived before him, and they all remembered the day when they had been taken like livestock—though they hesitated to talk about it. They rarely mentioned their capture by rival tribes, men and women in exchange for hundreds of pounds, the rows of five boarding the ship, the lashes, the stench of fear and rage and despair, as well as the violent desire to die right then and there. But what they did share were distant memories, as if these still-young men and women had lived two lives within a single life. Scenes of daily life filled with moments of happiness that would never return: the fishing and hunting trips, the scent of grilled game, the lovers' quarrels, the slaps and bursts of laughter, the dance steps and heaving breasts swaying to the sounds of the drums, as well as the lovers' hips bumping against one another in defiance of an exquisite suffering. They would also think about the wars, the slaughter, the irreparable grief and abuse, the sighs that escaped their lips: combining everything from life, to create a bouquet that made separating the weeds from the chaff impossible.

Pierre the tinsmith and Bocar, known as Jeannot, who had both been in the colony longer than he, would occasionally tell stories of revolts, poisonings, delegations from France, betrayals and retaliations. He would listen to them eagerly, trying to understand. As for the stories about torture, he didn't need Pierre the tinsmith or Bocar to understand what that was about, because he carried the marks of torture on his body and had seen women and men, victims of the worst atrocities—his very flesh linked these stories to the institution of slavery. They all carried the evidence on their bodies, whether visible or not.

Sometimes, he would become confused by the stories of his friends. He had been told that he had likely arrived on the island on one of the last ships to make the voyage, just before the explosion of the uprisings. The only thing he knew for sure was that less than two years after his disembarkation, taking advantage of the Bois Caïman ceremony, the one that set everything in motion—fleeing the workhouses, the torture, the chains—he had sought refuge far away in the hills. Besides, at that time Cap-Français had hundreds of inhabitants—too many people around him. He needed to be alone before jumping into the fray. And all these languages resounding in his ears would become entangled and make his head spin. Sometimes he thought he'd recognized a word and would turn his head, only to meet an absent look, or a mocking or aggressive one. Then with the passage of time, the words entered him, mixing in with those from long ago, just like the hills that insinuated themselves in his internal landscape to create a somewhat hybrid and eerie world, frightening or comforting depending on the hour.

Some stories had taken over his imagination. A few weeks after his arrival, Zinga had a fever for four days, and he had been ousted from the workhouse so he wouldn't infect the others. The old negress Joséphine, who watched over the slaves who were ill, making them swallow herbal teas and lotions, had spoken to him about Makandal. At the time, he wasn't fluent in the language of the Creoles, and all the talk about the bonfire, about a sorcerer who had morphed into an insect to escape the villains, seemed to him a tall tale like the ones Pa Tadjou would tell them around the fire at night, long ago. Wide-eyed young children and youths would huddle against each other, holding their breath so that each word could make its way into their dreams. The adults, too, allowed themselves to be swept up in this magical moment and would beat their hands and cluck their tongues to mark the highlights. For the sick and the maimed too damaged to work, Joséphine would tell stories in which her weary mind, confusing eras and places, would create fanciful elaborate tales that beguiled them. But as soon as they left Joséphine's hut, when the surgeon ordered them to go back to the workhouses, or the fields, or the big house, the gruesome reality would soon overwhelm them.

Zinga the African cast his eyes on the increasingly distinct figures that were bustling about below, near the big house. The sun was about to set just like that; he could tell by the tint in the air that night would soon come. It was the same back home: the sun rose early, and the women got busy in the budding dawn, with each movement saluting the sun's arrival. And at the end of the day, the sun disappeared most abruptly with hardly a transition, as if to mark its absence even more. Zinga had heard a young man of color, fresh from Paris, who talked about how the sun set so late there that on his first day he wondered how he was going to fall asleep. In the market, he had bored them to death with stories about the wide boulevards, streetlamp lighters, luxury shops that sold green silk fabric, and furniture so refined and elegant that no one could sit on it in good conscience. So, they all remain standing, says Samuel the maker of cheap junk. And everyone burst out laughing.

Laughter was a part of their lives—occurring at unexpected moments even amid the most dreadful situations—out-of-the-blue, spontaneous maybe but always full of defiance and relief. It was a subtle warning that startled some. The disappointed young man of color had moved away from the group of blacks, sellers and resellers, buyers, women in search of a charm necklace or scarf, the healers and those without work—a whole little world milling about the Sunday market in Au Cap. Most of them came from so far away, from lands so remote and landscapes so diverse, that together they formed a sort of immense mosaic embedded between the hills and the sea of this island.

So much had happened since his arrival in Saint-Domingue. After running away from the plantation, he had settled in the hills with others like him who refused forced labor and instead were growing vegetables and provisions, selling them in town or exchanging them whenever possible for other goods. And sometimes plundering other vegetable gardens. Like when there were still many plantations surrounding the city of Au Cap. Always worried about drawing attention to himself, he would often offer his services to unload and load merchandise at the port. This also allowed him to watch the ships, which fascinated him and drew his attention. It was as if by watching the dozens of vessels of all kinds at berth, he'd get closer to his point of departure. It was as if he could glide along the waves and let himself be brought back to the place where he came from. Some Africans hated the sea smell because it reminded them of the ship's hold, the brutal separation, and the profound emptiness of the abyss. But he let himself be lulled by the delusion of making his way back from the opposite direction. At times, even the idea of hiding in one of these vessels headed for France and continuing to his native land would cross his mind—even though he knew it was impossible to retrace his steps. Since then, he had learned the name of the ship on which he had arrived on the island. Originating from the Zaire River, by way of Nantes, the ship *The New Society* had dropped him off along with three hundred men, women, and children. Now that he understood their language, he repeated this name like a slap in the face.

Some told him that he hadn't truly experienced slavery, having escaped less than two years after he arrived. He, and the others like him they called "New Negroes," had been thrown in a hut so they would get used to the climate, to the voices lacerating their skin, to the chains awaiting the first transgression, to the whip winding itself between fingers to strike faster and harder. All this so that they wouldn't catch the fever that was taking the island by storm, so they wouldn't catch the anger hiding in the four corners of the fields, nor the desire to flee that slows the steps in anticipation of finding the path to freedom. Yet these weeks of adjustment didn't produce the desired effect. First, he got fever, but as soon as he got off the ship, Zinga had decided to escape because he knew that otherwise his life would abandon him—unable to remain chained.

After his escape, Zinga still spent some time in limbo, as if his body had not yet decided to let this new world become his own. He met others like him, halfway between despair and stupor, in a space where suffering treads without noise—other than the sound of a thumping heart. He had seen faces that resembled his own, the worn-out eyes, the pursed lips. Pierre confirmed that one year before his arrival on the island, the whites brought over 25,000 Africans, but many had perished during this period, as if the brain had ordered the body to go numb forever. Zinga had no problem believing it when he remembered the jumbled shadows formed by the bodies of his shipmates, the heavy steps that reluctantly tramped this land of unknown mountains at the end of the crossing. He knew that, like him, many carried within themselves a need for freedom that grew stronger every day. Like a light whose rays slip through the fissures, the holes, and the cracks, in sync with the anger unleashed by the avalanche of memories, depending on the person, depending on the pain. One day he'd heard a white man declare they shouldn't allow the ideas of liberty and equality from the metropole to come to the colony, making their way into the heads of negroes. As if the enslaved men and women needed someone to tell them that they wanted to be free. Today, this need was bursting open like a forceful stream, spreading fear and panic among those who thought it possible to imprison the fierce beauty of human beings in sugar or coffee mills. It seemed Zinga had arrived on the island just before the end, that soon it would be over, and no one would be able to enslave them again—yet the irreversible pain was still pounding within him. He had been captured, tied up, and brought to this land that he got to know with the part of him that so wanted to live; but the part of him that was filled with memories still echoed in him, breaking his spirit.

Zinga stopped for a moment, as if guided by instinct. Now used to peering through the growing darkness, his eyes scanned from the east to the west of the plantation, the workhouses, the huts, the big house. He thought he glimpsed a multicolored reflection threading its way between the mills, and, like a frightened bird, Zinga's heart beat wildly.

In the first days of the crossing, Aza didn't realize that she was pregnant. The violent wish to melt into the foam of the waves preoccupied her so much that she ignored the nausea, fatigue, and wounds of shame in the same despairing heap. It was a woman with a pierced nose and a cold stare who, three weeks after their departure, set her knowing eyes on Aza's breasts. They were already swollen, hardily defying gravity, which emphasized even more her thin waist and full hips. Instinctively, Aza then touched her slightly rounded belly. Shutting her eyes to feel again Mali's caresses on her skin, the strong and tender fingers traveling the length of her legs and disappearing under the folds of her boubou, and filling her contented and consenting sex. On that day, he had placed a cajoling hand on her bottom and had pushed her forward so that she would join the other women who were walking toward the river. She had turned back to look at her man, the one with whom she had learned of the body's intoxicating fury, the one who could make her laugh and cry at the same time—like a hot sun when it starts to drizzle. With her still relaxed hips, hesitating legs, and lips full of his smell, she hadn't wanted to leave him. That was their last encounter. Mali must have had to wait for her for a long time, deep in the heart of the savannah. She had accepted the fact that they would never see each other again. According to rumors that had made their way to the village, no one would come back alive from the voyage on these large ships. Though their spirits undoubtedly would return to the lands of their ancestors to dissipate into thin air, to rediscover the trees they had known as children, and to rest in the lakes' waters. On the large ships they were surrounded by the sea—volatile, now violent, now calm, now blue, now grey. Still shocked at having been captured, Aza had seen men and women throw themselves overboard, letting themselves be carried away by the currents to embrace its deep waters. She thought of doing it herself, but in the end couldn't decide to make disappear the child they'd created, her and Mali. She kept her hand on her belly—all that was left of him.

By the time they were dragged out of the ship, Aza had already felt the baby move, a small furtive movement like the flurry of a morning breeze. She knew that she'd do anything to protect the baby. When she disembarked in Saint-Domingue, the surgeon who examined them noticed right away that she was expecting a baby. The negotiations lasted a little longer. The merchant demanded more money for both the mother and the unborn slave. One planter rejected her from his lot, undoubtedly foreseeing the reduction in earnings and the inevitable work stoppage in the months ahead. The planter Boulet, on the other hand, was thinking about the extra slave he'd acquire by including the young pregnant woman in his lot, but undoubtedly he had also seen the firm shapeliness of her legs, the brazen curve of her hips. Everything about her attracted him: the rounded belly, the long leg pliant like a solid and smooth vine, the neck held high despite the tears that filled her eyes. Her radiant, black face was framed by her short hair. Having brought the young woman back with him, the planter Boulet kept her close to the big house.

Completely enchanted by the regal manners of the pregnant woman, Boulet safeguarded her as much as possible. He decided that Aza, also called Agathe, had to regain her strength so as not to lose the baby and, for him, so as not to lose his investment. Then he decided that her rounded belly would not allow her to toil in the workhouses because she had to avoid miscarrying at all costs. He had her work in the kitchen on minor tasks. After giving birth, which went rather well, according to Ma Toinette, the most reputable midwife of the region, Aza was allowed to stay with the baby beyond the usual three weeks before taking up her work in the big house. The planter Boulet announced that he had paid dearly for this slave and had to protect his investment.

All her life, Aza had taken her beauty as a natural phenomenon in which she could wrap herself, like a comfortable, familiar boubou. On this plantation, where her life as a captive suddenly boiled down to knowing how to prevent other great misfortunes from befalling her daughter, she learned to use it as a weapon. Boulet was getting desperate. Behind the placid face, he couldn't see the woman's intelligence, but his heart was overtaken by her mysterious aura and became even more enchanted. His visits to the small room where she stayed with her daughter increased. The more she seemed accommodating, the more he felt the need to seduce her. Her body folded itself, melted under his own, her long legs wrapped themselves around his back, her hands pressing his backside, but a sound never escaped her lips. She invented moves that he would never have thought of. Even while bringing him to climax like he had never done before, Aza managed to increase the distance between them, and Boulet didn't know what to do to make her belong to him. He felt powerless even when his stiff member hammered her relentlessly. Sometimes he straddled her violently and deluded himself into thinking that he dominated her by orgasming inside her. Aza became pregnant by him less than a year after Désirée's birth, and she had a painless birth of a stillborn baby. For a long time, she cried in silence for this redheaded small being who seemed not to have resisted death. This loss strengthened her determination to focus all of her means and energy on protecting her little girl, who was growing up carefree, unaware of the destiny that would be hers if she, Aza, didn't intervene.

Apparently accommodating, it was during this second pregnancy that Aza began to make demands on Boulet, proposing them as favors that she lobbed in direct response to his persistence. Her first request was approved immediately even though it elicited many comments. They hadn't seen many young wet nurses before, but the planter Boulet didn't let the criticisms of his friends change his mind, nor did he care about the outraged looks of their wives, or the furious mumblings of the *ti blancs*, small-time white planters, or the muted sneers of the negroes on the plantation. Why did Eugénie Boulet accept her husband's decision? Some negroes said she didn't care at all because she couldn't take any more of Boulet's gambling passion, which was rapidly depleting the profits from the coffee plantation. In fact, Eugénie's expensive tastes had already sent her into the arms of a wealthier and wiser man, who, in this case, was a powerful merchant in the city. In the end, she left for Nantes with him, taking along her two daughters.

This is how Aza became the official wet nurse of the plantation, with responsibilities for the children over two years old. Every morning, she did the rounds, collecting the youngest ones after they'd been breastfed. The mothers would return at noon to get them for a meal of cassava and porridge, then at two in the afternoon Aza went to collect them again until the end of the day. After having carefully observed the ways the plantation operated, she had calmly requested the job of wet nurse, which would allow her to care for her daughter herself. She hadn't anticipated that her heart would also grow attached to the small beings with whose care she had been entrusted—a heart that she thought had closed like a dried-up spring. Every hint of a fever, a small shiver, a stiffening of arms or legs, panicked her. Ever vigilant, she was on the lookout for all the signs that threatened these little ones while their parents worked in the fields or in the workhouses. She had learned to pick out the chiggers and give a good washing to their hair to get rid of lice. While washing the small, lifeless bodies and wrapping the corpses, she had learned to recognize the symptoms of the deadliest illnesses: tetanus, jaw joint disorder, blue baby syndrome, tuberculosis.

She never shed any tears, but her entire body stiffened as if she were taking in some of their suffering. The day when Ma Toinette had laid the lifeless body of her son on her chest, she knew that misery was still following her and would always find a way to make her suffer, even when she thought herself immune to it. She let out a deep scream, then became quiet, gathering her silent sobs into a lengthy sheaf of anger and suffering. She kept the memory of the small brown body like a weight she didn't want to shed. She wouldn't try to get pregnant, nor did she do anything to prevent it from happening either. Her body seemed to have accepted the inertia that had become part of her, doing nothing to interrupt its course. She would pamper the children of devastated mothers who survived illness and despair, although with a heavy heart because after the age of ten they left her either to go to the workhouses or to join the house slaves in the big house. On some rare but tragic occasions, the children were sold beforehand, which plunged the parents in an abyss of pain that left them sealed off from everyone. She would do everything in her power so that her daughter, the daughter of Mali—the tall man with a supple body—would experience some happiness, even if meant putting up with the unbearable weight of Boulet's arrogant stupidity.

As much as she could, Aza took care of herself with the passing years, not for the sake of vanity but to keep Boulet. Every week—that is, from the time when Désirée could still be found in the hut in the mornings!—she would scrub her daughter's body as well as her own with leaves of vetiver and *medsiyen*, a medicinal plant, to chase bad omens and clever spirits. She had planted a white laurel in front of the hut. To get rid of the weight of Boulet's body, she would bathe in bay laurel leaves and place rose water in the creases of her breasts. Yet, the diffused sadness did its work in her; it pulled all over, softening her bottom, roughening the palm of her hands, drying out the skin of her thighs. Hardened by time, the torment had rooted itself in her, darkening her eyes. For many moons, her memories had returned only through impressions that filled her with a despondent softness: a bluish wind and the strength of black arms, the tenderness of a smile and the glow of a wood fire. The first time she burned herself, it was an accident, an act of frustration because she could no longer recall the timbre of Mali's voice. The memory would resonate painfully in her in a to-and-fro movement; it would cruelly let her go, and the more she pursued it, the more it seemed to flee. Crouched in front of the cauldron in which the leaves of citronella were tightly curling, she had raised her enraged fists against time, against oblivion, and in a dazzling moment of suffering, the brutal contact of the cauldron against her skin brought back the sounds that she had long sought. The singular voice returned with its sparks of desire and tenderness. On her forearm, there remained a small mark invisible to most people that she would caress sometimes, without thinking, as she would hold back at the corner of her lips the smile that was buried deep in her heart. Since then, she had left marks on her skin eleven times. On her left calf, there was one made in the hope of retaining the color of her mother's eyes, whose brown, sweet look abandoned its momentary task to follow her with affection. It was like a shiny brown chocolate, coming to her like a gift—and so as not to lose it, she had let the candle's wick lie against her skin. A tiny scar that shone in the dark when she passed her hands over it. In the same vein, waking from a dream both cruel and exquisite that brought Mali's body back to her—a pleasure so sharp that she was left panting—she had put drops of burning-hot oil between her breasts. She had bitten her lip so as not to scream from the pain, while feeling a familiar, long-forgotten warmth on the inside of her thighs. She respected each mark of complicity between her body and her memory. The pain that accompanied them at the beginning heightened the sought-after impact; afterward she simply had to control the suffering, avoid infections, heal the sores, let her skin adapt to the new scar. Then to dodge overly persistent questions from Boulet: refer to clumsiness, blame unruly children's reckless movements, and complain about harsh and burdensome domestic chores—all the while getting him used to the new mark.

Yet, over the years Aza realized that she might never bring Boulet to do what was most at stake: to get him to free her and her daughter. Over time, she had to accommodate his demands, channel them toward what mattered most: to keep her privileged position in order to protect her daughter. She knew that he had tried once or twice to go to other newly arrived negresses, or to Creole or mulatto women with long braids and coppery skin, and that she, Aza, could have found herself in the workhouses or in the fields. Hiding her anguish, she had chosen her strategy, enticing him then letting him leave, then taking him back with an indifference that derived from the genuine revulsion he inspired in her. With each separation, every time he returned, the man's fits of helpless rage against her body showed her the magnitude of his obsession. On the verge of tears, he would sometimes blame her for her sterile womb since the baby's death, and would look at her with suspicion and anger, then he would violently pull her to him and take her nappy, short-haired head into his hands, covering it with kisses. She accepted the violence of his hands, the bites on her breasts. She always remained quiet, consenting and docile, knowing that the more violent he became, the more likely he'd be ready to grant her requests. He would always return to her arms, simply because she had learned to make him believe that she wasn't waiting for him. When she wrapped her long body around his, when she used her lips, her fingers, and her entire skin to excite him, when she welcomed his sex with slow movements that made him tremble, she would always close her eyes. She would retreat to a faraway, silent world where only the dry wind of the savanna could reach her. Except that with time, the savanna became farther and farther away, she couldn't find refuge there anymore, and Boulet's unleashed jerking against her hips made her body shudder in disgust. And sometimes tears heavy with weariness would seep through the rim of her eyes, and she would pass her light, trembling fingers over her burn marks.

Inside, she shuddered to think he'd find out how much repulsion he provoked in her. Only Boulet's unconditional devotion could guarantee her daughter's future. She didn't have the means to buy their freedom. Besides, there was a law forbidding the freeing of slaves by their masters except in extreme circumstances: an attachment of the master to a slave who had saved his life or the life of his family or who had done a similarly exemplary deed. Having experienced none of these circumstances meant having to submit to the planter Boulet's clumsy outpourings, to his breath that was supposed to be seductive but was merely projected exhalations emanating from an owner's desire.

At the very beginning, after his wife's departure, Boulet was carrying on openly with the tall black woman, taking an obvious pleasure in brushing against her arm in front of his friends. Impassive, Aza listened to the planters' conversations, her mind obsessed with getting information to improve her daughter's status. She knew that the *ti blanc* Gillot, who was the steward of planter Martineau, Boulet's good friend, had had a son with a mulatto or a quadroon woman. Gillot's son, without a home or any means, according to Boulet's friends, had impregnated a negress before leaving for the eastern side of the island. "This child has no future. It will be a griffe, a poor white griffe on top of it." Then they'd roar with laughter. Inside, Aza refused to accept this complicated hierarchy that attributed epithets to people according to their connection to a white person: mulatto, quadroon, griffe, *mamelouque*. When the young mother was struck with eclampsia and died shortly after giving birth, Martineau had suggested entrusting the baby to Boulet's plantation wet nurse. Was he trying to free his steward from any parental obligation that would interfere with his work, given that he was already so lazy? Or was it just a last trace of his humanity? Aza had just given birth to the stillborn baby, and her breasts were dripping a sad and sweetish milk nonstop, like the tears she wouldn't shed. After many objections, muttered with contempt—"What kind of future could there be for a motherless little griffe? A poor white man on top of it, he would be just like his father, an unscrupulous man"—Boulet had yielded to his friend's insistence. He handed over the newborn baby, named Guillaume, to Aza. The young woman had laid eyes on the baby, who extended, instinctively, his small, wrinkled fingers toward the woman. She would raise him with her daughter, Désirée.

I'm flying. The mountain is so beautiful, it caresses me when I open my arms wide, telling me its secrets. With her, I am at home. I can reach the sun and the clouds. I can climb trees and I sometimes fall asleep, nestled in its branches. I look at the people below—like ants in search of a piece of sugarcane, a mango peel, a little drop of rainwater. I'm fine up above, waiting for the daylight to change. The sun's disappearance always surprises me, even when I'm expecting it. It's as if the sun were tired and closed its eyes in the evening. I also close my own, then open them again, and below I see small blinking lights, torches from the big house, candles, wicks soaking in oil in the small huts, the lanterns that make their way from hut to hut, from one plantation to another.

Once I went down to see all the faint lights moving like fireflies. I'm not afraid of werewolves. They don't have big shoes that make noise at night. And besides, I've never seen any and I love walking at night. The night lets out the animals that don't want to sleep. I want to see everything, hear everything. Day and night. Guillaume tells me to be careful of people because they give me a look sometimes. And in Ma Aza's eyes, I see that she's afraid for me. Yet all I do is take in my surroundings. I'm only trying to hear the sounds of the outdoors and to dance with my friends.

When I speak to other people, I get the impression that they don't understand much. I love telling stories to children, talking to Ma Aza, Guillaume, Bashira, looking around the workhouses and the fields. I don't like to hear the children cry; it hurts too much. I don't tell Ma Aza because she would be even more afraid. Once, I told Guillaume that the children were afraid, but he shook his head, then he said: "Shh shh, little sister, don't say anything. Shh, you're speaking too loudly, don't say anything."

One night the drums woke me up. I heard them beating like the wings of wild birds about to take flight. I jumped down from the tree and followed them. I didn't really need to see where I placed my feet, the earth was flying with me, we were both going fast. All around, faint lights shone like the sparks from a big campfire. I got close to the fire, I slipped in, amid all the bodies; I dance, I jump, I'm pushed by a woman's hand, I bend over, I touch the dirt covered in ashes and put some on my tongue. It itches. I smell blood, an animal's blood, an animal that screeches and howls. I don't like the cries of animals that are being killed. On my way back, I went by the river and dove into the water. The water was cool, I lay on my back, and saw the sun slowly rise. I dried myself with the sunrise, blood was running down my legs, so I had to wash myself again in the cool water. My blood, the very first time. Did the animal's blood make my own flow?

Ma Aza's eyes were wet when I told her. She took me in her arms, and I felt that she was happy but that her bones shook with anguish. I wanted to reassure her, tell her that I was fine, that she shouldn't be afraid, that in my head, everything was clear. But when I tell Ma Aza that nothing will happen to me and that I'm not alone, instead of calming down, she becomes almost ice-cold and puts her arms around me, without speaking. So, I don't say anything else. Besides, my blood never returned after that day.

The first three months, Ma Aza didn't let me out of her sight, and then she'd feel my belly. Finally, she called Ma Gaspard over. Right away I smelled the odor of moldy, dead leaves, the smell of a stagnant swamp. Ma Gaspard coated my skin, then asked Ma Aza to bathe me each night for seven days, using the leaves she had left. I ran all the way to the river, and I threw in the leaves. I washed myself in the cold water. I don't like dead leaves. I only like the ones that rustle when I touch them.

The blood never returned again. I don't know why Ma Aza is worrying so much. I on the other hand have no interest in having to wash blood-stained underwear every month. I saw the older girls in the big house do it. They hide, but everyone knows why they go to the corner of the stream that's the farthest away.

One morning, I overheard Ma Aza speak to Ma Bashira. She was trying to convince her friend that the planter Boulet would protect me. But I know very well that when he sees me, *Drooping Mouth* turns his face inside out. The children and I don't buy his smile that droops like a rotten plant. I feel that his lips must leave a slimy mud trace on the skin. Drooping and dirty. *Drooping Mouth* sends sidelong glances my way, but most of the time, I stay away from him. I hate his steps, the same ones that so often enter our hut and creep upon Ma Aza's bedding. As soon as I get a whiff of his smell of white wine, though I cover my ears, his movements are in my head, under my gaze. The children are restless, they're afraid. They tell me to hide, to hide them, and we close our eyes, and plug our ears. Sometimes I plug my nose too, but his white wine smell glides on me. That's why the children and I wash up so often. In the river, behind the hut, the water is fresh, cool sometimes, and our fingers become all wrinkled. But rainwater is our favorite; when it springs from the sky and falls on our hair, the rain cleans us—taking away the noise, the sounds, and the odors.

As if to give her even more importance in the eyes of the negroes on the plantation, Désirée, who was conceived in Africa and born on the land of Saint-Domingue, came to life in the middle of an immense storm that uprooted an acacia tree and destroyed three huts. Some were already asking themselves how Aza managed to protect the baby in the abominable conditions of the slave ship. When women disembarked from the ship, what faint breath remained in them was often too weak to sustain another human being. Those who had been captured or bought already pregnant had sunken eyes and ravaged wombs. Not only did little Désirée attach herself to her mother's womb despite the monstrous conditions of the crossing, but at three months old she remained alive despite the tetanus epidemic that had killed three newborns on the plantation. She was born well, people said. She was ritually bathed and well protected. It's undoubtedly because her mother had baptized her with the name Talfi to place her under the protection of the gods, in addition to the French name that the planter Boulet had imposed and that had pleased Aza when she understood its meaning.

While she was growing up with the other children under her mother's care, the myth of Désirée's invincibility in the face of destiny grew as well. Some thought it was the presence of the little girl with huge eyes and long legs that protected her mother. They said it was because of her that Aza obtained the position of guardian and was exempt from the exhausting work of the workhouses; that it was Désirée who brought her mother benefits from the planter Boulet, who was charmed by the little girl's magical aura. For they had also reached the conclusion that Désirée could predict the future, that she was born appointed. At six years old, she'd announced in a nonchalant tone that the cook was going to break his leg, all the while skipping as usual. The following Sunday, he was run over by a cart and broke his left leg. Aza did her best to keep the rumor mill, filled with danger, away from her daughter. She knew too well how things could easily turn from envious admiration into hysterical fear, and lead to the stake. The negresses accused of witchcraft became victims of torture and were accused of all kinds of crimes. Aza skillfully channeled the comments about Désirée, focusing on her spontaneous nature, her way of looking like a recently escaped bird, wings spread wide. That may be why, over the years, Désirée became like a wisp of a girl, a cricket, a hummingbird: the girl who people would see pass by, would hear sing, and whose ethereal breath people could recognize, but who never stopped long enough for them to be certain of her presence.

Désirée would frolic around the plantation with the other children under Aza's care, visiting the workhouses. Fascinated by the large, glazed piece of masonry where grains were placed to dry, she would run her bare toes through it and would also dip her fingers in the small circular basin for washing coffee beans, before being chased away by the negroes working in the workhouses. From time to time, she would appear in the yard where Aza was watching the children under her care—Désirée would either embrace her or curl up around her legs, nibble one or two ears of roasted corn, then leave again with Guillaume, the young griffe following behind.

One day in February, the girl, who was barely thirteen years old, came into the hut in a tizzy. As usual, she began telling a long, convoluted story that Aza couldn't get to the bottom of as the girl got more and more lost in the narrative. Impatient and worked up, she became confused by the words, but on that day, Aza understood immediately what she wanted to talk about. Guillaume was crouched down next to them, with eyes already filled with horror and curiosity. The whites had executed two men, two tall negroes with lighter skin, a bit like Guillaume. They wore neither shoes nor hats, only a shirt with a rope around their necks. Both were on their knees, each holding a wax torch. Aza stopped the child's rushed story. "You shouldn't have gone all the way into town and most of all, you shouldn't have watched this spectacle." She was imagining the torment of the stretching of the bodies of these two freedmen on the wheel, their bodies quartered, the dislocated body parts, and shivered in horror. "But why, Ma Aza, why? They killed them just like that?" Guillaume muttered, and the young woman saw the same question in the bright eyes and direct gaze of her daughter, who obviously would look elsewhere for answers if she wouldn't provide her with one. So, Aza took a few of the details that she had gathered from the planter Boulet, who loved to talk of this and that with her, even when she met his words with silence. On her end, she would get more information at the Sunday market, filtering through the details that she could use to her advantage. With an inner sigh, she asked herself how to explain to the children the conflict between the colonists of Saint-Domingue and the mulattoes who wanted to be allowed to vote. Aza at times felt very far from this struggle. How does one fight for one group and forget the others? How does one seek to enjoy certain rights, but refuse those same rights to others? She knew that the struggle between the colonists and mulattoes was just one part of the big fight. *Maybe it's me who can tell the future, and not Désirée like the negroes here think*, she said to herself—*but I think that there will be blood shed on this land*. How could she protect her daughter and Guillaume, this adopted son that she had nursed herself? Aza chose her words with care. Could she tell the children that Mr. Milord from the Provincial Assembly had announced to Boulet that for these two freedmen he wouldn't use the scaffold reserved for whites so that it wouldn't be sullied with the blood of the mixed-race while Guillaume's café au lait face turned trustingly toward her? Could she tell them that the severed heads of these men would be mounted on posts, that Ogé's head would be on display on the road leading to Dondon, and that Chavanne's would be found on the way to Grande-Rivière?

Aza knew that her daughter's liveliness and her insatiable desire to see, to hear, and to move about often placed her in danger. Désirée swallowed life in big gulps that seemed to beat from within, looking for a place to exist. What did she retain from everything that she took in? Sometimes, she rejected the dross so bluntly and so naturally that no one seemed angry. This is what Aza told herself for now! Despite her efforts, she couldn't keep Désirée in a cocoon, and even if she refused to believe what everyone around her was telling her, whether with malevolence or with honest sympathy, she knew that some of the rumors were true. Désirée seemed to be afraid of nothing and walked around everywhere, in defiance of the natural elements, the rules of men, the fear of night, and her mother's prohibitions.

On the night of the big ceremony hadn't someone seen a tiny, slight figure sneaking its way through the trees? The fleeting flash of two big, shiny eyes had crossed the area, some swore it. Even in the heat of the action, the wild glow of the fire, the noise, the chants and incantations, some asserted the next day that they thought they'd heard the slight voice of the young girl. The day after this long night, Désirée got her period for the first and last time, because it never returned again. On this topic, rumors were rampant. The most malevolent ones were saying that this girl was cursed, while the big-hearted, trusting ones said that she was blessed, and the rest said that this was another sign of her quirkiness.

Powerless, Aza followed her daughter's escapades. Sometimes, she would imagine her with Mali and herself in the savannah, watching as she ran like a brown gazelle with a hearty laugh, happy at the sun's impatience and the wind's sting. But here danger awaited them, here on this land that she couldn't really like, because it would always be the place where her life had become a nightmare. It was a magnificent island with majestic trees and mountains, but she couldn't reconcile the sky's beauty with what they had to endure on the land.

Désirée was not yet fifteen years old when Aza admitted to herself that not only would she never be able to discipline her but that it would difficult to shield her from suffering. Her bare and unprotected heart made her very vulnerable, and every wound could destroy her. When Virginie, a girl somewhat younger than Désirée, disappeared, Aza knew that this news would upset her daughter. It was impossible to silence the men and women in the workhouses, friends of Caleb, who was Virginie's older brother. He would repeat the details of the story relentlessly. Spirited and impatient, the young man, wanting to live freely, was collaborating with groups of insurgents and preparing to join them.

And he had promised his younger sister, whom Aza had cared for for many years, that he would leave with her. Caleb gathered food, weapons, and ammunition for his escape. Or at least that's what the plantation's overseer said when he brought over the constabulary. Who had revealed Caleb's plans? In which ill-intentioned ears were they planted? When the constabulary came to arrest him, accusing him of attempted assassination, he objected, kicking like a pureblood refusing a harness. Afterward, witnesses said that the gendarmes hit him to subdue him, that he fell violently, his head struck a big boulder, and the bleeding didn't stop. Caleb died less than an hour later. When Virginie didn't return, Aza sounded the alarm immediately. Everyone knew of the strong bond that had united the brother and sister since the death of their mother. The next day, Virginie's lifeless body was found near the river. The doctor said that she had drowned. Did she try to run away? To go where? Did she want to die? Aza watched as her daughter's eyes sank into an abyss of despair from which she could not rouse her. Her body limp and calm, Désirée let herself be embraced without saying a word.

A little while after the tragic deaths of Virginie and her brother, Aza's quiet and tenacious persistence compelled the planter Boulet to secure a place for Désirée in Madame Gertrude's sewing workhouse. The following month, Aza had to face the facts. Despite her daughter's fascination with fabric, she'd never be a seamstress. Her imagination made the three other young apprentices smile, and sometimes Madame Gertrude herself got caught up in it. Désirée loved to caress satin, she'd laugh when she saw silk shimmer in an elegant and whimsical way, and would rub against the cotton or twirl it around her, depending on her mood, not following any guide. Between her fingers, the scissors became like two birds that would slash long, multicolored bands. A few days after the large Bois Caïman ceremony, Désirée wrapped a red sash around her waist. Over time, she added other colors.

Some negroes called the young man "Ti Griffe," as if to show that they knew where he had come from. After being weaned from Aza, his wet nurse, the child went back and forth between the two plantations. His grandfather, Gillot, Martineau's steward, was happy to order him clothes and get him a tutor when the time came, without showing the least affection toward the young boy whose light-colored eyes resembled his own. Instead, Gillot complained of the expenses he incurred and how worried the boy made him, although it was the planter Martineau who acted as if he were the elder relative and who took care of most of the expenses. "This guy Gillot will never be anything but unscrupulous," said Martineau, who despised the *ti blancs,* the low-class whites whom he thought were lazy and irresponsible. They couldn't be trusted, and he was convinced that his steward was stealing money from him, though he had no proof. But the planter had a soft spot for Guillaume, whose lanky appearance reminded him of his youngest son—and he couldn't bring himself to let Guillaume's grandfather go.

Despite their very different backgrounds and personalities, Désirée and Guillaume almost never fought. As children, they were inseparable. The boy, who was less than two years younger, adored the girl and would often follow her on her wild treks which led them very far from the plantation. He had a hard time getting used to her capricious pace, running into her back when she would stop in the middle of a race to pick up a stick that she'd turn into a bayonet to attack imaginary enemies. Likewise, he had a hard time finding her when she would hide during an impromptu game of hide-and-seek. She would emerge from the leaves of a tree or from the corner of a cave—and all he could do was laugh when he caught sight of her. As for her, she respected his need for solitude and didn't bother him when he didn't answer right away.

In fact, as a child Guillaume had spent more time on the Boulet plantation than with his grandfather. Aza was his adopted mother, the one who had wiped his nose, applied suction pads on his body when a bad cold almost took him away—it was in the swirl of her skirts that he found home. The smell of verbena on her body, the light touch of her fingers on his cheek filled him with happiness when he would seek refuge in her. But she almost always had a little one beside her, in her arms, against her chest, on her knees, at her feet, pressed against her hips. Always. Sometimes he was jealous of it—he who never knew his mother. But the others for the most part went back to their mothers at the day's end, except for the terrible day when a mother had been sold without her child. As for Ti Griffe, he had never had another parent but this good-for-nothing low-class white planter who should have acted like his grandfather but instead would only grumble when he saw him. And his godfather, the planter Martineau, who would tell him stories about the blessed time when the city of Au Cap, the "Paris" of the colony, shone with life: concerts, plays, cabarets. Martineau would say, "My wife was still alive then and we'd often go to shows." They had seen *The Marriage of Figaro* a short while after it premiered in Paris. The Martineaus' library was one of the most extensive in the city because, as he explained to his godson, they would buy the books from planters who had decided to leave the island permanently and sold their assets before boarding a ship to return to Nantes or Bordeaux. Madame Martineau loved reading and was even a member of a book club. He was proud of his wife. She wasn't like these snooty women who would come from France and whose only thought would be to strut around—with empty heads and greedy hands. Martineau's eyes would sparkle when he revisited the good old days; then, returning to reality, they would fill with melancholy.

Typically, the Martineau plantation's atmosphere exuded discontent, anxiety, and sadness. This prosperous owner, who had settled in Saint-Domingue for almost fifty years, had for some time only three words on his lips: Return to France. Not for trips lasting a few months, which, as a rich white planter, he could afford—but for good. Besides, his children, who were settled in Bordeaux, did not intend on returning, and he missed them terribly. The colony was terrifying him more and more. He would mutter constantly about the terrible events that were going to happen, that he wouldn't simply stand idly by, waiting to be massacred at his advanced age. He had fought enough with mainland commissioners who meddled in everything without understanding anything about life in the colony. They issued decrees, ordered measures that had in the end served no purpose except to make the planters' work more difficult, though the colony was making France richer. It was no longer worth withering here, fighting off the blows from the corrupt and ineffective colonial administration that was unable to defend the planters' concerns. Now here they were having to fight the mulattoes and the freedmen too. He had nothing against the mulattoes, but some lines shouldn't be crossed—because who could predict the negroes' reaction? What happened in August 1791 must be a lesson for all. The planters had thought they were safe, and yet the negroes had revolted, carrying on like savages during a ceremony that Martineau considered satanic. More than a thousand whites had lost their lives. And so many plantations destroyed, burned down. Though it's true that Martineau's plantation had been restored and he still managed to turn a profit. The workers—or "cultivators," since we must no longer call them slaves—became more and more lazy, whining and making all kinds of demands. No, now he was seriously thinking of returning to France. Guillaume knew by heart the planter Martineau's tune, which he would keep repeating to his visitors.

Visits from one plantation to another were becoming more and more stormy. Guillaume would sometimes overhear animated discussions among planters in which the words were expressed in different tones: "colonial assembly," "human rights," "freedom," "settler interest." Conversations in which sarcasm and anger, indignation and terror intertwined. Some could not get over the abolition of slavery—even if many former slaves had returned to the plantations and were working under the same conditions. Then the planter Cordier, the more aggressive of the two men, would retort, "Except they were spending more time on their plots of land." After talking about the black cultivators, he'd go after the people of color, who, according to him, posed a real threat. Then he'd rant about the decrees and measures that the metropole wanted to impose on them, even though France was in no position to protect their lives and their properties. The colony enriched France. France owed them protection and security. Though they shared some of Cordier's positions, Martineau and others who were not as extreme took offense on principle because of Cordier's authoritarian tone. Cordier, after all, had only settled in 1760, profiting from the rising popularity of coffee. And then it turns out he had political ambitions, wanting to set himself up as the settlers' spokesman like Martineau, whose family had settled in the colony for more than fifty years, and who had experienced so much tumult that he could have written his "Memoirs." Silent in his corner, Guillaume could predict Cordier's reaction. The latter considered Martineau's and his friends' lax attitudes responsible for this chaotic situation. Groups of insurrectionists were active almost everywhere in the colony, especially in the South, where the situation was alarming, according to what he had heard. And now the insurrections were spreading to the North. The metropole was debating whether to adopt an effective strategy, showing itself weak by negotiating with savages like this Toussaint Louverture who was, after all, a slave like the others. Swept up by the paranoia that seemed to take over some planters, Cordier said it was time to be done with the "Society of the Friends of the Blacks" and all of this philosophy that encouraged rebellion. He even asserted that these emissaries were en route from France to teach the negroes how to revolt. From there, the discussions were ignited. Not daring to express his opinion, Guillaume knew privately, from his contacts with the cultivators, that they were not waiting for an emissary to come from France and inject them with the need to revolt. He also knew that it was thanks to the work of blacks on the plantation that France had earned more than 135 million livres from Saint-Domingue in 1788. Curiously, no planter made reference to this during their discussions. Normally, these discussions ended with a brouhaha of discordant voices, and then the planter Cordier would leave, raging. When the young man ran into him on the streets of Au Cap, Cordier would look him up and down with arrogance or pretend not to see him.

Guillaume could never forget that he was a griffe, a low-grade half-breed. At some moments more than others, he felt like he was floating like a balloon too heavy to fly very far, but also unable to touch the ground. He would remain suspended between different worlds that seemed to reject him. With his light complexion, his grey eyes—inherited apparently from one of his grandmothers, whom he never knew—and his thick red hair, he experienced his mixed-blood status in the flesh.

One day when he was still very young, he'd stopped playing with Désirée to ask Aza in a small voice what "mixed-blood" meant. The term came out of his mouth with some loathing, almost as much loathing as would pierce through the voice of the big white planters. Aza drew him close to her to answer his question. Mixed-blood, she said, in a calm tone, looking at both of them, one after the other: Désirée, long and strong, with bright brown eyes, and Guillaume, markedly paler, smaller, frailer. She punctuated her words with a half smile, so rare that it seemed divine, which she reserved for the children and her friend Bashira. "When you cut your finger last week, Guillaume, what color was your blood? And you, Désirée, when you hurt your knee, what color was your blood? And the planter Boulet, when he had a nosebleed last month, what color was his blood? Red, right? I've seen no mixed-blood." So, in a gesture so swift that her mother couldn't stop her in time, Désirée got hold of the knife that Aza was using to peel potatoes and made a cut in Guillaume's hand. While the boy, still in shock, was appalled as he watched his blood gush forth, Désirée made a small incision on her left hand and with determination seized Guillaume's hand and brought their hands together so that the two wounds could stick to each other. She watched as the drops of blood soiled the fine gravel that Aza had gathered to make a small enclosure at the entrance of her hut and passed her bare foot over it, mixing the stone's blood with the ground and weeds. Mixed-blood, she said with a burst of triumphant laughter in twirling her skirt, and then led Guillaume in a crazy race.

Désirée's presence in his life didn't necessarily make things make sense, but it did embellish everything, as if the colorful gaze she imposed on her surroundings reflected her light. In her presence, he had the impression of dancing, as if her mere silhouette infused the air with lightness. Sometimes, he worried about other people's wary reactions—blacks, whites, mulattoes, or griffes—and would have wanted, as Aza did unconsciously, to hide her from the eyes of others. To place himself in front of her, protect her from the world's stupidity. But can a flame, a moonbeam, or a bolt of lightning be hidden? He also thought that the one he called his little sister was special, and he admired her as one would admire a gem, a luminous day in the rainy season, an unexpected rainbow, a shooting star that you alone can see.

Once he turned fifteen, Guillaume no longer asked questions about the meaning of life, even in the most difficult moments. A loner, he didn't react when people called him Ti Griffe, whether it was full of malice or not. It was just a subtle reminder of his condition as a métis with no guaranteed resources. Being métis was one condition that sank him despite the encouragement of Aza, who had the ability to detect his anguish even when he hid it under the cover of a soft, quiet appearance. Would his godfather be leaving for France, as he had been threatening to do with each report of a new fire, or the latest skirmish, or recent attacks by the rebels? What would become of him then? Would his grandfather still be the plantation's treasurer? Gillot was already threatening to change neighborhoods, on the pretext that his pittance was useless. He, too, was thinking of going on the eastern side of the colony and finding his son, Guillaume's father. Would he take Guillaume with him or would he leave the planter Martineau in charge of him? Would Martineau throw him out of the house before leaving for Bordeaux, since he would be leaving soon? Guillaume felt the weight of this situation—the situation was deteriorating on all sides, and already two neighbors had joined the list of settlers who were fleeing the colony. The planter Boulet seemed to not want to leave. Would he be willing to house Guillaume? He knew how to help, and despite his young age, he could replace the treasurer if necessary. Aza would be on his side and would defend him if needed. During the insurrection, Boulet's plantation had been spared, no doubt because it was much smaller, located high up in the hills, or maybe it was plain dumb luck . . . Of course, the negroes on the plantation had whispered that Désirée's presence had protected them from the insurgents. Without saying it openly, Boulet had thought the same thing. Guillaume had seen him look at Désirée in a troubled and troubling way. He had also caught the same worry in Aza's eyes, which must have been also reflected in his own. Indifferent to the stares of others, Désirée had done a pirouette as she sang one of those mournful songs that she'd picked up from the workhouses through which she often passed, but always in a flash.

Guillaume would have loved to have the same carefree spirit as his "little sister"—he was the one who was constantly getting all worked up. How does one make one's way in this turmoil that was bubbling up all around? He remembered when groups of insurgents invaded the Martineau plantation, ransacked the remaining furniture, and set the huts on fire. Bashira had come to get him, thrown a dark garment on his back, covering his head and his fair hair with it, then roughly pushed him out of the house, ordering him to go find Aza. He was eleven years old, and he had already learned that his skin color could mean his death. He had silently cursed his light-colored eyes. Terrorized, tripping over stones, he had fallen, he had run, a sharp pain in his side forced him to stop often, but the fear of machetes was stronger than the pain. He soared through the dark, automatically taking the path he'd traveled so many times before when playing with Désirée, fearing the darkness but knowing that it was to his advantage. When he arrived, his legs lacerated by thorns, his body trembling, Aza was waiting for him at the door and embraced him.

During the days following the insurrection, he'd stayed safe in Aza's hut, with the smells of the fires invading his lungs and his nightmares. At night he stayed awake, unable to move, his eyes wide open until dawn. Once he was able to return to the Martineau plantation, it was to be fully immersed once again in an atmosphere of terror. Some whites spent their time telling stories about the torture and the horrors that rebel slaves had inflicted on their former masters. The negroes on the Millet plantation had raped the planter's wife, five of them taking turns in front of the husband. Then, having killed the husband, they raped the woman while she lay on her husband's dead body. On another plantation, they had bound a carpenter on two trestles and had sawed the man in half, as a group watched the spectacle while laughing. They'd burned down houses, killed hundreds of animals, cut off white people's heads. These rebels showed their true nature, displaying the range of their savagery that no one, not one person, could forgive. This was proof that they had been right to keep them enslaved, since barbarians like that needed to be handled. Sometimes, very shy voices objected. Some settlers had also tortured their slaves! Had they forgotten the horrors committed by Caradeux? And what about on the plantation with that overseer by the name of Odélus, who only cared about increasing profits, not thinking about the high numbers of negroes who were dying there? Was it surprising that this Odélus was executed by the rebels? Most of the time, these objections were either unnoticed or roused virulent protests and even barely veiled threats. Quickly enough, the protesters would quiet down. Almost all of them were thinking about Fernand de Baudière, this old white man from Petit-Goâve who was accused of being the author of a petition written by the people of color in the city. The crowd had dragged him from the prison where the constabulary had put him, and he was lynched in front of everyone. He served as an example of the fate reserved for those who displayed their anti-settler sentiments.

After the insurrection, the planter Boulet took in survivors for a few weeks. Hailing mostly from the same region of France as himself, these planters, small merchants, stuck together, protected each other, and gave work to their lower-class relations. The planter Martineau would make fun of them a little, but he also trusted the "network of provincial settlers," as he called them. In fact, the plantation's surgeon came from the same part of the country as he had. The events spread panic among the group, which had scattered all over the place. A few left after the revolt, avoiding the risk of being "massacred by the savages." Others escaped to the Spanish part of the island, or just went back to France, while others were happy to send their family back, but they themselves remained to oversee the plantation. Then, a while after the big ceremony, Toussaint Louverture had ordered the reopening of a number of plantations, and Martineau's was part of the group. And life seemed to pick up where it had left off, but not as before. Much had changed, according to what the accountant, who was constantly filled with a special rage against the freemen and the blacks, would tell his grandson.

During these days of insurrection, many small-time whites lost their lives, and Guillaume would ask himself once again how his grandfather had managed to escape the carnage. On the other hand, the surgeon was captured and had to go with the rebels. The supervisor as well as the carpenter and the mason, who by a terrible coincidence happened to be there repairing the cupboards, were all killed. All small-time white planters, the kinds that the negroes called bad whites—as if they had had their skin bleached but were not actually real whites. Whities. The kind who don't speak well, who looked dirty all the time, who ate whatever they could find, who went from neighborhood to neighborhood, who were employed by the important whites for all kinds of menial jobs. And sometimes for the underhanded blows that the planters gave to each other or to those who were plotting against the colonists' interests. Suspicious fires, poisoned animals, unexpected ambushes—some *ti blancs,* poor whites, were willing to do it all for a few pounds. To buy land or a stall, to pay off their debts, to keep a demanding mistress happy. As an adolescent, Guillaume would spend time with his grandfather and his friends. He saw so many small-time white planters and could recognize them by their vagrant bearing, their carelessness, and their sometimes vulgar way of talking. Deep inside, he looked at them with disdain and shame because he himself knew that his grandfather was like them, and so was he by association. Or maybe he felt that it was worse for him since he wasn't even a real *ti blanc,* he was two rungs below them on the ladder. A griffe. Twice small: *ti blanc, ti griffe.* Education was his only chance, the fact that his godfather, who often thought about his two sons, let Guillaume enjoy being in the house and even hired a tutor for him when the grandfather declared that he no longer saw why his education mattered. Martineau encouraged his desire to write, and above all he gave him books to read. Thanks to him, Guillaume had taken accounting courses and worked as the administrator's assistant. He didn't want to be Ti Griffe his entire life, and often an immense despair would make him taciturn and sullen.

In these moments, feeling profoundly melancholic and outraged, he would write poetry that he would then either hide or rip up depending on his mood. The poem that he had written for Désirée, his "little sister," he had slipped into the pages of a copy of La Rochefoucauld's *Maxims* that Martineau had given him for his eighteenth birthday. It was with a smile tainted with the hint of subtle humor that he had slipped his poem to Désirée into the pages of this book:

> You, girl of gestures fanciful and beautiful
> Who on a rainy day filled with sadness
> Creating an appealing expanse of playful gladness
> Make us see in life the gems most truthful

The baton hissed above my head then passed by my left shoulder with the same speed, brushing against my cheek one second later. I barely dodged it, made a thrust I'd learned, and struck him after two attempts, which the master blocked with little effort. He saluted me, then grumbled, "Not bad. My little Marie. Keep at it!" Master Silo had been saying these same words for months now, after each training session. But I had seen his half smile, and that was enough to fill me with pride.

I knew I was far from having the master's skill, because in my eyes he was the best among those who trained the insurgents. He didn't need to attach *mayomba* amulets to the baton, he could hurt someone, maim someone, kill someone, or simply warn someone as he pleased, without poison or talisman. His baton was a part of him; sometimes the wood seemed to come from nowhere and I would see it spin rapidly, creating around Master Silo a halo of movements that were impossible to pin down.

I lay on the grass damp from the last rain and stretched my stiff limbs. With eyes half-closed, I let the wind breeze through my smock and breathe in the mountain air, the enchanting smells that came from the orange trees. I had to take advantage of my hour of rest before returning to the encampment. Above, the sky's fawn colors signaled the end of day. My turn to be on the lookout for Moussa's group was about to start. I got up in one bound, having learned to restock my energy in a short span of time. I felt reinvigorated, as the breeze had once again washed over my spirit and camouflaged my fatigue. I needed to be alert because I had to go to Boulet's plantation and get news of Désirée.

Having patrolled so many of the nearby hills, having bent down so much, carried pails and loads of all kinds, my body had taken on a strength that made me proud. Along with its frailty, my body had lost its naïveté from the early days of its arrival on this island. I liked the feel of my strong and firm limbs, hardened by the comings and goings on the hills and the skirmishes with enemy troops, whether they were other groups of negroes or groups of Frenchmen. This land had become conquered territory. It's always easier to love what is familiar. I'd developed a relationship of trust with these hills. They hid me, they protected me, they fed me, and one fine day without my realizing it, they became mine.

Arriving in Au Cap when I was eight or nine years old, according to the shipping ledger of the first plantation where I washed up, it's as if I had spent the first years learning how to perfect my survival techniques. Even before training to handle the baton, I knew I had to be strong and not quit. An old negress who had been watching me for a long time told me two days later: "You're one of those who've decided to live. You bend your body and your mind, that's great, my girl. But be careful to not lose yourself along the way, my little one." First assigned to work in the laundry in the big house, I was then quickly sent to the workhouses, where my reputation as a rebellious and impertinent little negress child preceded me. The reprimands, the blows from the riding crop, the unwanted fondling followed me to the sugarcane fields, where the overseer finally decided to let me go. Me, Little Marie to Master Silo, Marie Nago to the others. My memories from before my arrival in Saint-Domingue were becoming more and more blurry. I had only vague, mysterious impressions that got mixed up from time to time with more recent experiences. Undoubtedly deep within me, my name from before lay dormant, waiting for me to decide one day to dig around in hopes of finding it, but I had no desire to do so. I had accepted my life on this island, in these mountains that had become a part of me, as if some of this red, humid earth had taken root under my skin, permeating it with its smells and its mystery. I had chosen to live and to live here.

A few weeks before the 1791 uprising, I had run away from the plantation and joined the insurgents. I will never forget the first time I met Moussa's group. An Ibo negro, who probably took my youth for naïveté or weakness, was the first to pin me against a tree; beaming, he moved his big hands on my breasts as he tried to slip his tongue in my ear. I kneed him where it hurts, then stuck a finger in his eye. A witness to this scene, Moussa, who was leaning against a tree, burst out laughing and told me that he was taking me into his group. I hesitated for a second before accepting the offer, because I knew that this Ibo negro was going to take revenge before long. I had to be on my guard. I didn't hold it against him. Some men, whether free or enslaved, sometimes think that they have the right to satisfy all their desires on women. But I had decided a long time ago that I would be the one to choose who could touch me. In any case, the Ibo negro died in combat in the next skirmishes with French troops.

I really liked the life that I made for myself. I had settled in the hills with two other young women, who, like me, had run away from the workhouses. Bayi and Elsa took care of the plot, and we sold our vegetables in the Sunday market. I was the one to sell them because that was my responsibility. The few months spent in the big house had taught me how to behave so as not to attract attention to myself, inviting the evil glances, the informants, the *ti blancs* searching for compensation, the free blacks who behaved sometimes worse than the whites, the mulattoes, whom we had to watch constantly because they wanted to replace the whites, and the other former slaves who also had to survive. I had learned to trust my instincts and navigated my surroundings carefully, under a show of smiles and friendly banter to sell my wares.

It was Sunday, several weeks after the fire that had destroyed almost the entire town of Au Cap, when I saw Désirée for the first time. We could still smell smoke in the air, and people's wan faces carried signs of nights filled with anguish, flight, and lit torches. So many rumors were going around about who had done what, about who was to blame. Was it the commissioners Sonthonax and Polvérel, or was it Galbaud, the newly arrived governor who apparently didn't like mulattoes? Or was it the rebellious slaves released from the prisons by the commissioners Sonthonax and Polvérel, given the threat of the men working with Galbaud? Who committed the most atrocities—Galbaud's partisans or the others? Were the men of color the ones responsible for this fire? In any case, two-thirds of the city was set on fire. I went to the market hesitantly, because anger, fear, and mistrust were still floating in the air. But we had to sell our vegetables, stock up on provisions, and get information. I was immediately attracted to this long young girl, whose eager look seemed to swallow the objects and people surrounding her, though without lingering too much, like a child who couldn't wait to learn more and didn't stay in any one place for fear of missing out on something. Instead of walking she skipped, her arms floated in the air, even her lips were moving—with the hint of a smile or a peal of laughter always on her face. She'd stroke fabric with frail fingers, quickly touch a piece of fruit, would lean on a stand nonchalantly, and would disappear a minute later. Only to reappear next to a carriage, as she caressed a horse with one hand, while pulling gently on a donkey's ears.

While my eyes were following her movements, I immediately felt other people's distrust, the malicious or fearful glances cast her way. There was an empty space around her, along with jeers and offensive comments. It's funny how I, whom people considered to be self-centered, felt obligated to get close to the young girl and to protect her. It's undoubtedly because she seemed so unaware of other peoples' reactions, and because her eyes lit up as she looked at the trees and the flowers, and because she surrounded herself with many colors. I felt that she also loved life. I placed my hand carefully on the child's shoulder, because she was still young, as I realized while watching her closely.

"I also like horses."

She tilted her head toward me, with an astonished and happy look. "Yes, we shouldn't be afraid of horses. They're nice. Do you hear that, Gilles?" and she turned her head to the left. I looked at the empty space, perplexed, but she offered no explanation. She spoke in a slight voice, and passersby turned to look at her. Instinctively, trying to deflect attention from her, I started to bargain with the fabric seller, while leading away the one whom from then on I took to calling "the little one."

I didn't understand where this strong protective instinct came from. I had enough just to care for myself, to stay alive while all around me death prevailed, despite the sun and the wind, despite this sky so blue that sometimes I wanted to breathe it in.

I would smile and make jokes without getting too attached to people, because the spirit of death was roaming all around us. Elsa would say that life wasn't giving us many gifts, but that we loved it anyway. Bayi added, "Cruel mother." We then burst out laughing, but I smelled death's odor more each day. The battles were endless. The population of former slaves refused to work under the same conditions as before. Everywhere the cultivators complained, ready to fight to stay free, to get a piece of land, and to be at peace. Was it too much to ask for? But I could tell that this was not going to be easy. I was living day-to-day, ready to face death. I couldn't take care of anyone else. That's why I took all necessary precautions to not get pregnant. How could I take care of a baby in these conditions? Once, I had acted without thinking, letting myself be carried away with desire, with the moment's joy leading me. With Basir, I forgot to be careful, to count the number of moons, and I let myself go. It was such a special day, the day after the big ceremony. I was barely sixteen, according to their ledgers, of course. On that day, I realized that I could never stop fighting. My body knew it before my mind did. That's why my body started to get strong, in preparation for battle. On that day, for the first time since my arrival on this island, I felt free. It was dawn and I was leaning against the trunk of a mango tree. I was curiously very calm while the drums were still beating, and the grumbling uproar and feverish atmosphere overtook the hills. Basir's footsteps had led him all the way to me. I'd been imagining this moment for a few days, since he'd looked at me in an innocent way that fooled no one. We slowly made love, both enjoying each moment, savoring our bodies, honoring our movements as if we were welcoming the arrival of dawn. Without rushing, because time was just another element we had to control. It belonged to us and we were going to bend it at will. I didn't get pregnant. It may be that my body was unable to bear a child. Too much emptiness, too many mornings where hunger lodged in corners, leaving only empty grooves where nothing could sprout. Many girls who came from elsewhere like me or others born here can't bear children. The elder Ma Freda could do nothing for them: her potions, her massages, her incantations, could do nothing for the traces left by the horror in our minds and our bodies. Just like this Désirée, with her unique destiny. A child from here and from over there. A Congo girl, a Creole girl.

Nago was added to my name to distinguish me from the other girls named Marie, who were also baptized to make it quick and to honor a Virgin whose sad face never earned my trust. I am Marie Nago because I came from over there. But in the end, there are as many Marie Nagos as there are Marie Ibos and Marie Congos. I met two other Marie Nagos, one in the workhouse of the Courtil plantation in Limbé and the other at the market. I've since learned that the one from Limbé lost her life as she was giving birth to her fourth child. I'm sure other women, undoubtedly dozens of other women like her, have lost their lives somewhere on this island. Dead or alive, with one fewer limb, with markings on their backs or on their faces. When I explained to Désirée why I was given my name, she burst out laughing and said: "Well, I'm Désirée Congo." I wanted her to understand that it wasn't the same, and that she couldn't call herself Congo, but then said nothing. Why did I want to keep her "unique" while I relish the feeling of seeing so many women with my name in this land where we have been dropped? So many Marie Congos, both similar and different, tall and slender or small and stocky like me, head wrapped or hair cropped, jacket wearing or skirt wearing, loud or quiet, unexpressed anger or a happy face, with children on the hips or with a womb sterile by choice like mine. This comforts me sometimes. We don't look like each other, but we are the same, because we've taken this name on our backs and undressed it, then when the name became stripped, we rode it.

In fact, on that day Désirée had been persuaded by what seemed to her to be the best argument, which convinced her to add the name "Congo" to her own. "You wouldn't really want me to be called Désirée Boulet?" she asked with eyes that foretold a story that I knew was a sad one before I even heard it. I think that was the day that I understood that this young girl was special and that it was my duty to protect her.

Jérôme Beauvais adjusted his collar one more time, a nervous gesture that he couldn't control. Would he be able to match his older brother's dispassionate haughtiness? It's true that Julien was a white man, the son of a woman from La Rochelle who died six years after his birth, who had benefited from his father's fortune and gone to France to continue his studies, then decided to settle over there to escape the increasing waves of dissent that were washing over the colony. But he, Jérôme, knew that his future was in the colony, even though he had studied in France like his half brother. His father expected him to take over the management of the plantation. Despite the constant rancor he felt toward his father, a resentment that his older sister, Sophie, judged irrational and even petty, he had to admit that the planter Beauvais didn't shirk responsibility for his two mulatto children. Aware of the bad faith behind these thoughts, Jérôme nevertheless thought that his father's care didn't ensue from an authentic attachment to these métis children, it was merely an extension of his love for Mathilde. Already the widower of his La Rochelle wife, the stern and sour-faced Beauvais had bought a group of slaves from a fellow planter who had decided to return to the metropole. Mathilde, washerwoman by trade, was part of the group, and Beauvais, to the great surprise of his circle, was seized by an almost savage passion for this woman originally from Senegal. Sometimes, despite the mix of contempt, rage, and pain that this image aroused in him, Jérôme would tell himself that his father must have raped her, at least at the beginning. He suspected that Mathilde undoubtedly felt some affection for this man with whom she had lived for more than twenty-five years, and he'd been angry at what he considered to be a shameful surrender. Jérôme would have liked to find more rational motives to explain the unease he felt toward the couple formed by his parents. And besides, he realized that he felt no respect, no tenderness for them. A part of him held them responsible for this unpleasant situation, at times painful and full of frustration, in which he found himself as a young métis man in Saint-Domingue. Confusedly, he also was angry with Julien, though he was aware that was unfair: not only had his older brother not had anything to do with their father's decisions, but as an only child for ten years, he had always shown a sincere fondness for him and Sophie. In fact, only their sister, three years older than him, was charming in Jérôme's eyes. The birth of Sophie, a little adorable girl "the spitting image of her paternal grandmother," had undoubtedly helped to validate Mathilde's status, because soon afterward Beauvais had freed his companion. At that time, this was typical enough. Jérôme was fully aware that the same thing wouldn't happen now. He knew that things had changed in the colony and that mixed-blood people had to fight harder to keep their privileges.

Sophie would often tell him to forget that he was métis and to act like a white man. It's true that no one could guess by looking at her that she was a mulatta. Early on, she had decided to take all the steps to position herself favorably outside this conflation of mixed-blood people, with all these labels that only relegated the métis to a frustrating and marginalizing world. She protected herself from the sun's rays and with as much determination she avoided contact with blacks and other métis. Her white appearance allowed her to do this. Unlike Jérôme, who didn't know if he should rejoice or not over his darker skin tone, his brown curly hair, and his slightly hooked nose. Without a doubt, his appearance left him no choice but to accept his identity as a freed and mixed-blood man.

It had been two years since Sophie left for Bordeaux. During a trip to Saint-Domingue, the Bordelais merchant Paul Dandet fell in love with this young mulatto woman fifteen years his junior and married her without worrying about the fact that her mother was a negress. A few months pregnant, the young woman had left her family, the sugar plantation belonging to her father, to settle in France. Her last letter boasted of the advantages of her city life. The ideals of the revolution favored an atmosphere of fraternity and respect for human rights, she said. After a few months of adjustment, the Dandet family had accepted their Creole daughter-in-law. The fact that little Isabelle, Bordeaux-born, was even lighter-skinned than her mother made things easier. No need to shout their origins from the rooftops. In two generations, everyone would have forgotten that she had mixed blood in her veins.

Jérôme stopped himself from uselessly adjusting his collar yet one more time as he thought of his visit to his sister's house. Sophie, who loved him dearly, had encouraged him to visit them, but he soon realized that she regretted it somewhat. His métis appearance didn't make things easier. She stumbled on the word "brother" when she presented him to the family, stammered while trying to explain their origins, and to cut short her embarrassment, he made it a habit to proclaim himself to be "a friend from the colonies." Sophie's relief hurt, but he wasn't mad at her. Nature had given her the tools to escape; what right did he have to put a spoke in her wheels? After two weeks with his sister and her family, he left to meet Julien in Paris, in the little room where he was lodged.

A young adolescent freshly arrived from the colony, he marveled at the beautiful and immense capital city the first time he went. At first dazzled by the streetlamps, the sound of horse-drawn carriages on the cobblestones, the voices of different French accents, the women's clothes, the houses, he soon became disillusioned. His outings with his brother and his friends, then his solitary walks as a student, made him discover a more somber world, where misery, violence, and injustice coexisted with the opulence of the privileged. Jérôme saw the life of the poverty-stricken, the children whose eyes and dirty and patched clothes told the story of days without bread, cold days without heat, of beatings and poor treatment. Some pressed their filthy faces against the windows of the bakeries, before being chased away by the owners. Others rubbed themselves against the passersby, slipping expert hands in coat pockets or extending ungloved hands to beg for a few coins. Jérôme couldn't believe the threadbare clothes that people wore in the heart of winter, while he felt like the cold was icing him deep down to his bones, even though he was nestled in the large coat that Julien had given him. How did these unfortunate children manage to survive? The truth is that they died by the hundreds. One of Julien's friends, a pompous student, who was always strolling with a book or two in his handbag, confirmed that 50 percent of French children were dying before the age of twenty.

Back in Saint-Domingue, after his studies in the law, Jérôme had contacted other freedmen like himself, especially Claude Lavaud, the son of a friend of his father. Very involved in political matters, Claude would gather other young freedmen at his house, and the discussions were passionate and virulent. Jérôme didn't fully trust the two different types of discourse, which focused either on retaliation and battles or on betrayals and base acts. Either debasing ourselves in front of the whites or fighting like savages! There should be a more dignified way to settle the differences of opinion between whites and people of color. Nevertheless, he wasn't going to indulge in barbaric acts as the slaves had done in 1791, sowing the seeds of blood and terror. Besides, the risk of being executed like Ogé and Chavannes was great. It was important to be diplomatic and open to negotiation. In his opinion, this would be the least costly solution in terms of human life and the most effective one. He'd had enough of these struggles and these barbaric conflicts, but he realized that Saint-Domingue was heading for a bloodbath. Au Cap was becoming a desert that he no longer recognized, as if the violence was seeping even into the dust of the roads, the wind that shook the leaves on the trees, and the petticoats of the women—nothing seemed like before. A climate of war invaded the public places, giving the city a smell of catastrophe in the making.

The evenings spent among friends, the cocktails and parties, became rarer and rarer and often they devolved rapidly into arenas of discussion, and even arguments. He avoided them as much as possible. At the planter Martineau's house, where friends of his father's had brought him recently, he had met Guillaume Gillot, a quiet young man, who seemed to be a regular at the house. One guest had spewed heinous words against all the other groups, like the freedmen, the free blacks, the colonial administration, but especially against the *ti blancs*.

Despite himself, Jérôme felt personally targeted and humiliated. It was obvious that there were other mulattoes there, so why show this lack of courtesy in a discussion to which they were all invited? After having listened to the planter with an air of apparent indifference, the young man had taken refuge in the garden, promising himself to avoid these types of people in the future, since their words were too much like provocations. Undoubtedly, Guillaume felt the same way he did, because there he was, sitting on a bench, with eyes filled with gloom showing the feelings Jérôme had felt as well. "I'm one of those *ti blancs* that he was talking about," Guillaume plainly declared. Jérôme was not able to hide his surprise and Guillaume smiled, with a tired and wise look. But before the two men could continue any kind of conversation, a multicolored figure appeared near them. Jérôme moved back, instinctively, because the young negress who had come close to them was roaring with laughter and clapping her hands. When he saw her, Guillaume had smiled without being too surprised that she had appeared out of nowhere, acting with so much exuberance. In addition, she had done herself up in a rainbow-colored skirt, as if she had patched it up herself with pieces of shiny multicolored fabric. Around her slim waist, she had wrapped equally vibrant scarves which turned into a multicolored belt. After embracing Guillaume, she began to talk as if the two men weren't there. She seemed to ask and answer the questions herself in a bouncy and happy voice, then left as she had arrived, after planting a noisy kiss on the *ti blanc*'s cheek. Stunned, Jérôme couldn't keep himself from asking the question. "Who's that?" "My sister," Guillaume answered, a smile filled with affection transforming his face. Jérôme didn't think it was a good idea to ask more questions, filing away both the *ti blanc* and the negress on the list of people to avoid, but he held within him the echo of this winged voice, finding it curiously out of place in their world.

Cécile put down her book. She couldn't help but be concerned about Ferdinand's tardiness, all the while trying to hide her worry from her mother, who was already uneasy and was raising her head from her embroidery work at every sound. Having knocked on her husband's workroom door to prompt him to do something, she then asked the coachman to be ready take out the horse-drawn carriage. Of an anxious nature, Esther Lespinasse had become even more so during these last few months. The deterioration of the political situation in the colony, whether it was about the conflict between the mulattoes and the blacks, or bloody skirmishes in the South, or fires and other acts of violence in the city of Au Cap—everything left her nerves on edge. She would have preferred to keep her children at home, all the while knowing that it was impossible to prevent young people from following their own path. And her son's path seemed to diverge more with each passing day from what his parents had planned for him.

Her father's reassuring yet slightly annoyed voice reached Cécile. "Come on, Esther, one hour late isn't so serious. You know how Ferdinand is." Generally, Georges Lespinasse didn't appreciate the attitude of their son, who in his view was too often ready to have fun and let himself be led by his friends, and his wife's worry only increased his own disapproval.

Cécile gave an inward sigh. Their father would never understand his children's choices. Above all, he wanted Ferdinand to follow in his footsteps: to join him in the workshop and prepare to lead the family business, and when the time was right, to continue the tradition of high-end designer clothing by Lespinasse & Co. The young man thought only about his music, his compositions, which he played, either with fervor or fancy, for after-dinner activities and friends' parties. He would declare that his only two passions were music and women, that's what made him happy. Right now, he was supposed to be with his new mistress—a *mulâtresse*, a landowner not far from La Place. Ferdinand talked about her casually, but beneath his casual demeanor, Cécile knew that he was attached to this woman. A mere sixteen months separated the brother and sister, and their strong bond, which began in childhood, had been strengthened during their years studying together in Paris. As parents who worried about their children's futures, with much affection but no real consideration for their children's own dreams, Georges and Esther Lespinasse inculcated values they considered necessary to improve their status as free blacks in Saint-Domingue. First, education and work. Without neglecting the importance of Cécile's education, they had doubly invested in the education of their son, the eldest of the family. For them, it was certain that their charming and cultured daughter would find a free black man to marry. Someone respectful, hardworking, proud of his origins, aware of the difficulties and challenges ahead. If possible, someone not too involved in politics, but connected enough so as not to remain with arms crossed, watching as the gains from the struggles led by their ancestors were destroyed. An upright man with a backbone who'd be ready to maintain the privileges of their class, a man capable of remaining vigilant, especially about the mulattoes, who proved to be their fiercest adversaries. After all, Georges Lespinasse was the third generation of free blacks. His father, Marcel, was a free black through his mother, who had received her manumission for her services as a faithful and dedicated wet nurse and had worked relentlessly to buy herself a small coffee plantation. Over the years, Marcel Lespinasse had built a reputation as an uncompromising and inflexible master; the men and women who worked on his plantation could attest to it, but he was not embarrassed to make a profit from his business. For the last ten years, his oldest son, Emmanuel, who had previously been second in command, had proudly taken the helm of the plantation, adopting the same methods as his father. Pierre, the second-born, had made a career in the army like many other free blacks. The youngest son, Georges, had gone to France to pursue his studies and discovered by accident his vocation as a tailor. After an apprenticeship in Paris, having returned to the colony, he set up a boutique in Cap-Français. It had been twenty years, and the outfitter Lespinasse & Company had built a loyal clientele among the men who cared about their attire. Having successfully adapted the trends from the metropole to the Saint-Domingue climate, Georges Lespinasse competed with even the French tailors located in the city. For important occasions, the free blacks and the mulattoes would rush to his shop, certain that they could find an attire or a unique vest that reflected their tastes and peculiarities. Now it was Ferdinand's responsibility, as the sole male inheritor, to come work beside his father, to prepare to take over the business in a future that was more near than distant. Unfortunately, Georges realized that Ferdinand seemed more interested in wearing beautiful attire than in creating it. For a while, Georges consoled himself with the thought that his son would maybe follow in the footsteps of his military uncle. Having become a captain in the French Army, Pierre Lespinasse was a role model for many of the free black men who had chosen the army, even if sometimes they'd complain of their inferior status compared to the mulatto or white officers. Since the insurrection and the mounting tension among the different groups in the colony, the situation had become even more complex. The black officers were distrusted by their superiors. Pierre had discussed it with his brothers and thought more and more of joining the rebels, as the French called them. Georges had wondered if it would be a good idea for his son to join an army of insurgents, but when, as a last resort, he mentioned the idea of a military career to Ferdinand, he quickly understood that he didn't need to worry. The dumbfounded and slightly mocking smile that had met his proposition confirmed that his son would never entertain such an option.

Cécile told herself that, for her father, learning that his son had for the past six months been spending time with a woman—a divorced *mulâtresse* and the owner of a restaurant in town—would be a new source of disappointment. It was like a double betrayal. A divorced woman and a *mulâtresse*. She was a threat to Georges Lespinasse's aspirations to ally his family with another lineage of free blacks to consolidate their group, ensuring a proud and dignified reproduction of their own kind. He was already thinking about one of the Manigat girls from Limbé, whose family would appreciate the equally renowned virtue of his own family. That family, like the Lespinasse family, prioritized education and work. How many times had Cécile overheard her parents, grandparents, uncles, their friends, free blacks like themselves, repeat this same old tune? The whites had the colonial administration on their side most of the time, the mulattoes had financial resources that their fathers had left them, but the free blacks who were though Creole born on the island of Saint-Domingue could only count on their work and their education. As children, to amuse themselves, Ferdinand and Cécile would repeat to each other this old tune "The mulatto becomes free by sleeping, the black becomes free by working" without understanding the meanings that lay beneath these words. "Laugh, children, but one day you'll understand," their grandfather would say. As she was growing up, in her heart Cécile had always questioned this family saying and its repercussions. It was true that the mulattoes would often become free by the right of blood line or family line; while for the blacks, freedom rewarded a life of work. But should we always judge individuals by these criteria? In doing so, aren't we enclosing people in fixed categories that don't go beyond what is visible? But some ideas caused her family to feel waves of anger and emotions that reached so far back that Cécile, despite her rebellious nature, hesitated to face them sometimes. And she also admitted that the planters held firmly to the prejudice of color to justify slavery. For this reason, the mulattoes found themselves in a class that was both privileged and ambiguous; and the free blacks caused problems in relationship to the other blacks. It was an awkward situation at times. Cécile truly felt, for instance, that her parents didn't want to revisit the story behind their ancestor's freedom. It was a story with unfinished sentences, bits of confused silences, discreet grunts, and almost inaudible sighs. Cécile and her brother had learned to avoid these details, focusing instead on the story around the special day, the one on which their ancestor was freed, eleven weeks before her death. It's as if their ancestor had struck a deal with death to let her live freely for at least a few days before claiming her.

The special day was the day when Victorine Lespinasse received her freedom papers; her former owners had also given her their family name before setting off again for the metropole. A name that she gave to her son, whose father died six months after his birth. When decades later, Léger Félicité Sonthonax, civil commissioner of the Republic, "delegate to the French islands of America to restore order and peace," printed the slaves' certificate of emancipation, in declaring that "men are born and live free and equal in rights," the Lespinasse family as well as other black families spontaneously rejoiced. Afterward, more subtle questions arose, and an uneasy atmosphere settled in some minds. Some free blacks felt wronged. Disconcerted, Cécile sometimes discussed it fiercely with her friends. "How could you not rejoice from the fact that all men, all blacks are declared free and equal in rights?" The answer sometimes came with an ounce of resentment that the young woman found to be petty. "We all worked for it, we are educated, yet we are going to find ourselves at the same level as slaves—we are black like them and free like them as well. How are we going to distinguish ourselves from them?"

At twenty-two, Cécile often felt very old. Not only because her family was pressuring her to make a good match and get married. The atmosphere of constant struggle and tension among groups also weighed on her spirit. Sometimes with an amused smile, she would envy the calm attitude of her brother, whom she considered licentious since finding Fougeret de Montbron's libertine novel *Margot la ravaudeuse* in his room. He had undoubtedly forgotten to hide it in the special place that Cécile had never been able to discover. Curious, the young woman had leafed through the disparaged novel that her mother's friends would discuss in whispers and with reproving looks. Since then, she'd asked herself if some of them hadn't appreciated reading it. Despite herself, on the sly and with increasing anxiety, she had read some pages of the story of this girl who had a liking for "libidinous pleasures" and who was dying to "experience the sweetness of copulation." Just thinking about it made Cécile cross and uncross her legs. The thought of her mother coming across this book made her squirm even more. Where had Ferdinand found it? And most importantly, how did he dare bring it into the respectable—their father's favored word—home of the Lespinasse family? Two months earlier, she had run into her brother walking arm in arm with his belle. Cécile loved to watch him walk. He never seemed rushed, as if he were delighting in every moment: in a late afternoon breeze or in a fresh breeze in the morning, seeing the men and women who passed by in front of him, the voices that surrounded him—sweet and affectionate, surly and harsh, authoritarian and submissive. With each step, the soles of his leather boots sank into the dust, as if he were deriving an exquisite pleasure from it. On that day, he had warmly greeted his sister, and in a modulated voice like in his musical compositions, he introduced Emma: "The two women of my life: Emma, I introduce you to Cécile."

After the customary greetings, Cécile exchanged a few words with the young woman. Surprised by her bright eyes full of intelligence, amused by the smile at once shy and daring, she found herself smitten with Emma. Why did she unconsciously imagine her to be vapid, coquettish, and lazy even before meeting her? It was undoubtedly because of what was said here and there, among the whites, the slaves, and the free blacks. Just last month, at the birthday party of one of her childhood friends, she'd overheard someone announce her distrust of mulatto women because "they are always trying to steal our men." In answering, Cécile didn't mince words: "Should we be seeing men as objects capable of being stolen? In fact, I shouldn't be surprised. Some of us even own some slaves, human beings who don't enjoy their freedom and who belong to us body and soul." Of course, the hosts had complained about Cécile to her father, accusing him of not having raised his daughter properly. She should have known to remain quiet when she had opinions that called into question the heart of a system from which she was profiting! Didn't her grandfather and her uncle own slaves themselves? If she wanted to shock the good people, she should do it in her house, not in ours! . . . Georges Lespinasse had sharply scolded his daughter, without however daring to tell her that, with words like those, she wouldn't be able to find a husband. Deep within, he wondered whether he had done the right thing in giving so much leeway to his children and exposing them to the new ideas floating in the air.

By an irony that Ferdinand found absolutely delightful, the time and money invested by their parents in his education had instead borne fruit for their daughter. The young man mocked gabardine dresses, grey sheets, or the piles of taffeta in his father's shop; he would play the piano and wanted to spend all his time focusing on music. The only passion that could keep him away from women was the desire to create, to feel within the irrepressible tumult—between the tones that infiltrated his spirit and his hands—to finally see his fingers moving to give rise to a melody. So, he would spend hours at the family's piano, to the great despair of his father, while Cécile, for her part, would read everything on hand. She and her friend Angeline Maurepas had found a way to get books from France even if they took months to arrive. The young girls spent hours with their heads in books, taking notes, then having passionate discussions that amused and unsettled Ferdinand. How could two young women, so beautiful and charming, give so much importance to something so abstract? Angeline's older sister, a former student of the Religious Girls' Community of Notre Dame du Cap, had become the two girls' tutor when they were twelve years old. A passionate reader, Henriette Maurepas had instilled in the two young girls her love of books and words. Cécile's solid and beautiful friendship with Angeline started with their common discovery of poetry by Ronsard and Du Bellay and the discussions it inspired. Endless conversations, beginning with the giggles of embarrassed girls who were fascinated with their bodies, their desires, and their fears, and including discussions on the increasingly serious matters of love, life, and death. They grew up together, sharing their fears and moments of sadness, their laughter, and especially an unsayable and painful longing to be elsewhere sometimes, anywhere as long as it was elsewhere. When together, they would recite the verses of Ronsard, cry as they read the verses of Du Bellay, which Cécile found too morose, and laugh until they cried from reading Rabelais's stories, then they'd both sigh from this inexpressible aimless desire that would not leave them.

In spite of herself, one day Henriette told them about her night at the Convening, on the eve of the 1791 insurrection. She disclosed almost in a whisper how, like other young women, she had hidden behind the heavy curtains to look at Boukman's gangs who were screaming at the whites. The nuns trembled on hearing the screams. Some of the older young women had escaped at night, and in the morning told stories about the ceremonies, dances, and drums. The least brave packed in close to each other, stifling their nervous laughter behind their hands. Sometimes Cécile wondered if friendship could be summed up in a simple accounting of shared moments or, instead, if friendship amounted to feelings born of these moments. Among those whom she called her childhood friends because their families knew each other and met at parties and social occasions, she wondered who of them could she really count as true friends? Friendship meant sharing what mattered most with someone, without even realizing it; friendship was laughing together about the same silly jokes and crying when one was hurting. Friendship didn't mean talking about the latest fashion while sipping orange liqueur.

In observing her father and his assistant Mirabeau from a very young age, as they handled the scissors, sewed, and adjusted clothing on patterns, Cécile had developed her own tailoring skills. After creating dozens of dolls' dresses, she had clothed the domestics of the plantation, the children and the young girls, and finally the older women as well. Her mother, who was elegance incarnate, had gladly and proudly worn one of her creations. Despite himself, Georges admired how his daughter, in the blink of an eye, had been able to make from a simple shiny cloth an elaborate piece—somewhat bold in his eyes, but which brought out the client's best. He told himself that, in time, she could rival the famous free mulatto woman Grignotte, who made clothes for the wives of the freedmen, especially for the women of the army officers, both black and mulatto. During fete season, one could see the horse-drawn carriages lining up in front of her studio on Rue Saint Pierre, near the Comédie du Cap. For now, Cécile paid no mind to her father's dreams. She had built a clientele for whom she sewed if and when she felt like it. "You and me we're alike, little sister," Ferdinand told her one day. "You're following your passion, when all is said and done."

The nearby sound of her brother's voice greeting their mother made her raise her head. He had finally returned. Mother could relax now. And me too, she added with feeling, knowing that if anything ever happened to her brother or to her parents, she'd be destroyed. It would be great not to become attached to human beings because then, undoubtedly, we'd suffer less. It was of course this fear that also explained why, till now, she hadn't yet found a man to her liking. She had let Gauthier's son whisper a few sweet nothings but found him a little too much of a socialite to discuss serious matters. She looked at the youngest of the Magloire Ambroise clan with some interest, but his interest lay elsewhere. The young woman knew that with a little effort, she could have charmed the young man, but the catch was that she didn't have that little feeling that would have propelled her to act. The passion wasn't there. A former classmate returning from France had spoken to her about Jean Racine and had recited verses that Cécile had carefully written in her notebook. With many shades of meanings, a tingling sensation near the thighs and the breasts. She would often repeat them to herself for sheer pleasure: "I saw him. First, I blushed then grew pale. At the sight of him, my troubled soul was lost."*
The troubling images evoked in *Margot la Ravaudeuse* would also return sometimes. Meanwhile, when she thought about passion, it was the most concrete of passions that could be seen in the eyes and gestures of some couples she imagined. Especially the passion she had witnessed one Sunday after church services, on the market's main square. The two young people embracing, pressed up against a wall, half-hidden by a fruit and vegetable stand, were still. She hadn't seen their lips move. Only their hands gestured: the young woman's hands were wrapped

---

* *Phèdre,* by Jean Racine, translated by Margaret Rawlins (New York: Penguin Books, 1991), 51.

around the young man's waist, seemingly tracing a story on his back, with light and fine touches; the young man's hands embraced the young woman's shoulders, lightly caressing her body in a circular movement, sensuously and enchantingly. Cécile, standing in front of a nearby stall, had seen these two bodies bound together and this glimpsed passion made her dream, made her almost sigh. She and Angeline had spoken about love, about a passion that would be both wild and tender, insane and serene. Theirs was a love that would give them wings.

Suddenly, Cécile recalled once more the luminous smile and somber eyes of Desirée, the young woman cloaked in moving colors whom she had met in Madame Gertrude's sewing workshop and whom so many people had run across, seen, or glimpsed. Yet no one could explain her behavior or manage to stop her for more than a few minutes. This was a young woman with nimble fingers, but who was not at all interested in sewing. She would wrap herself in fabric, placing it around her head or her waist, enveloping her body, transforming herself into a rainbow girl with saddened eyes. Since the first time she saw her, Cécile associated her with a bird of multicolored plumage. Sometimes, Désirée would come by the Lespinasse shop begging for new scraps of fabric. Cécile and Mirabeau would gladly give her some, choosing the most silky and rainbow-colored ones. Georges Lespinasse curbed their generosity: You shouldn't encourage her. Go home, Désirée. Does your mother know that you're in town? Once, Cécile wanted to keep her longer in the shop to make her a dress, a ready-to-wear garment in nets of pastel colors that would fall in frivolous folds from the waist. But after a few minutes the young woman had fled, with a mocking peal of laughter. Cécile envied Désirée's freedom, even though she knew that there was something strange in the behavior of this young woman who was probably just two years younger than herself, but who seemed so young, enclosed in a child's world in which reality didn't quite have a place.

The young woman dove back into Olympe de Gouges's book, which Angeline had been able to obtain after many negotiations and feats of secrecy. The play was about the enslavement of black people. Cécile suspected that her father would be unhappy and a little afraid to see her read such a controversial play, not to mention the reaction of the colonists' defenders, who were also ready to attack anyone who questioned their privileges. Without a doubt, this play could never be performed in the colony. Even in France, it had made lots of noise, creating all kinds of furor and conflict. Without the support of the Society of the Friends of the Blacks, Olympe de Gouges would certainly have suffered grave consequences. In any case, at the theater, free blacks had to sit behind whites and mulattoes, in their own separate corner. In fact, blacks had been authorized to go to the theater only ten years after the mulattoes could. Some friends had straight out preferred to abstain. How does one get used to injustice? And yet, she often reminded herself that she was a privileged person, one who was born free while the slave ships were carrying men and women, crammed together like animals. In fact, until she turned six years old, the last ships were bringing these enslaved human beings. Coming from Congo for the most part, according to her uncle Emmanuel, who had bought a few of them. He has since regretted it, because it seemed that, even before reaching the plantation, some of the enslaved had run away to the mountains or to the ports. With the then commander's help, he had caught a few of them. Meanwhile, Uncle Emmanuel never missed an opportunity to complain about the losses incurred, which would trigger Cécile's indignation. It was becoming more and more difficult for her to have the most banal conversation with her uncle. Like other free blacks, he would pile on his violent words toward the whites, the mulattoes, and the formerly enslaved who had become cultivators with the abolition of slavery. Cécile sensed that the conflicts were intensifying, and before long they would explode. Anxiously, without wanting to say a word, she wondered what would happen to life in the city of Cap-Français.

Aza was also thinking that soon nothing would be the same. She seemed to be counting the hours, looking at the sky and clouds, listening to the wind swish through the trees, and sometimes her breathing would stop, a sigh too muffled to see the light of day. Yes, there would be changes, but what would they be?

Her friend Bashira would often tell her: "We're heading toward a new era, that's for sure. I feel it." It amused Aza when Bashira took on this prophetic tone—she, who believed in neither diviners nor sorcerers, neither talismans nor prayers. But she didn't argue with her because their time together was too precious to waste discussing things that she couldn't change. So, Aza let Bashira get rid of her weariness and sadness as well as her fits of anger and frustration in this way. It meant everything to her that Bashira remain present, within reach.

Sometimes, under the crushing weight of Boulet's body, she would think about Bashira. She'd think about this precious tenderness which they both relearned and which connected them. She had already been burning herself when she met the young woman with lips full of defiance and secrets. It happened a few years after her arrival. It was market day. Two pairs of eyes met, both full of the same despair planted in their limbs, both with the same memory of a lost elsewhere that remained like a muffled but never distant sorrow. It was a look of instinctual complicity, a rueful and fresh spurt, a tune from yesteryear.

She was aware that Bashira's presence in her life enabled her to put up with Boulet, whose slightest gestures irritated her and eventually disgusted her more and more. At the beginning, Aza and Bashira spoke very little, their lips hesitating while their two bodies were already creating a new language bolder than words. Intense emotions were concealed under the fringes of eyelashes or in the brushing of skirts when an unexpected request came from the planter Boulet, or when faced with insults from an estate manager. But also, intense emotions rose in vast swaths full of softness on moonlit nights; these nights would allow less bitter thoughts to filter in, along with memories mixed in with the present to render the moment more humane.

    Aza couldn't remember when their friendship veered toward the inevitability of physical desire. Oddly enough, neither of the two women had thought much of the stares of others—of their smirks, of some men's vulgar comments, of the obvious disapproval visible in the fold of some women's lips. They had received this good fortune with stunned, happy, and magical surprise. They smiled at each other even when they were apart, whispered to each other from afar as they waited for the next encounter. When the two women reunited inside the hut, they let their bodies come unburdened of the accumulated weight of sadness. Their hands recounted the moments that make one shudder even in the darkness of night because anger and shame can't hide under the cover of darkness. They were intoxicated by tenderness. Pleasure enfolded them both as they snuggled together, skin touching skin, hair entangled on exposed shoulders. Their sex complicit in the joy of their likeness, and a profound delight kept them pressed to one another for a long time. Palms enclosing a willing chest, the two women let the blissful silence chase the pain of suffering. Aza would forget the jerking desire of the planter Boulet, the brush of his hairy legs against hers, and the savage foul breath emanating from his lips. Aza's gentle kisses comforted Bashira, erasing the memory of the workhouse master's rough hands and the harsh orders he would shout as if they were insults. At times, their warm, urgent tears flowed and the hut would become a pristine, peaceful haven. But laughter is what often kept them close, body against body, with legs and thighs intertwined, with looks interlocking and buried deep in unsayable secrets. Laughter had returned to their lives. The tenderness that Aza saved just for Désirée, Guillaume, and the children was profound, intense, deliberate, and instinctive. Because of Bashira, laughter had returned impetuous, sassy, and priceless. With Bashira, she became who she was before the barracoons, Aza before the ship's hold, Aza before the chains. She became a happy young woman again, yet not too happy to recognize the existence of bliss like her former self long ago—but now, she was able to savor the present moment with eagerness and discretion.

For a while now, with a silent and profound grief, Aza had been watching the wear and tear take over her friend's body. It wasn't the slow and sometimes peaceful decline that occurs with the passage of time; it was a sudden and ferocious deterioration that offered no respite. The work in the workhouses had ravaged her cheeks, her arms, and her belly, which gave Bashira's skin the appearance of watered-down coffee that looks just like dirty water. For years, her heavy workload in the food supply workhouses, which were the most onerous ones on the sugar plantation, turned her nights into punishing sessions that sapped all her strength and allowed for a mere four hours of sleep a day. And when her muscles had withered, when her limbs could almost no longer function, Bashira had been assigned to another workhouse where the work was less arduous—she was like the crushed and broken sugarcane stem that's been scrapped as it decomposes. When they met, the young woman cut a dashing figure that seemed to defy fate. Today, she seemed to be shrinking with each passing day. Just once, a long time ago, Aza had suggested using her influence on the planter Boulet to get him to ask his friend Martineau to have her transferred to the kitchen of the big house, or to the laundry room, but Bashira flatly refused. This was her way to fight destiny, accept her scars, take them on fully, and send them back to Aza with a pursing of her lips that was more arrogant than a whip. Holding her curved back with dignity, her forehead remaining high and rounded, her eyes never lowered and full of light. Aza didn't make a fuss about it, but each time she saw her friend, a deafening sadness took over her entire body in the face of her friend's body that seemed to be getting closer to its own shadow. But Aza also knew that to survive without caving in, a person had to map out her own destiny. In bringing her looming despair under control, she increased the offerings of simple pleasures to Bashira: lemongrass herbal tea, a very ripe mango waiting for the satisfying bite into its yellow flesh, a swig of liqueur stolen from the kitchen. The moments spent together became even more precious, imbuing their gaze with an almost sorrowful brilliance.

Since the cultivators had more time to focus on their negroplots and their families, the two women would meet more often. Boulet seemed less possessive, and Aza enjoyed some breathing room to see Bashira more frequently. Bashira had adopted Désirée and all the children that Aza watched or had watched, and the little ones looked forward to her visits because she always carried sweets in her pockets. A special bond connected her to Guillaume, whom she had always protected from the negroes' mean jeers and the haughtiness of the whites on the Martineau plantation. Since the insurrection, Bashira and Aza met before, during, and after intense gardening sessions when they picked, cleaned, and prepared food for their own eating pleasure as well as for sale. They spent two days together at Aza's, two days together at Bashira's. With the passage of time, Aza had become expert in the growing of vegetables and would always prepare a large pot of soup that the two friends enjoyed after their work. Bashira had infused the area surrounding the plot of land with different mouthwatering smells. On top of the provisions that Bashira grew for herself and for selling, she had also planted an orange tree and a cherry tree and used them along with all the fruit she could find to make jams and fruit preserves. As for sugar, Aza had taken as much as she could from the big house for her friend. It always bothered her that Bashira, who had spent so many years wearing herself out in planter Martineau's workhouses, had to use raw syrup for these jams. Sugar and coffee were packaged and sent to Europe. So Aza would take sugar and other little delicacies from the rather limited reserves of planter Boulet, and if he ever noticed, he said nothing about it.

Together, they talked about everything and nothing at all, getting to what was most important in subtle ways, trivial incidents, veiled words or stories from their daily lives. Bashira had told Aza how they had replaced commanders with conductors, under the system of this Polvorel fellow who came from France, as if changing the sun's name made it less hot. The workers were supposed to participate in selecting the conductors. "That's just a way to keep us on the plantations, because all the decisions they take in their famous council undermine us. And when you don't agree with them, you have fines to pay, and if you can't pay them, you're imprisoned. Me, I knew from the beginning that it was still slavery under a different name. So, I left the plantation but stayed on my little plot of land. No one can chase me from there." The conductors, unlike the commanders, weren't supposed to use the whip or any kind of torture, but instead they had to try to persuade the blacks to be good workers. "In other words, don't rest too long, don't ask for wages, don't make too many demands, and most of all don't run away. What's more, we women receive less than men do for the same work. It's as if the sugarcane that I cut and that I grind doesn't make sugar!" Reaching this conclusion, Bashira let out a "tchweep" that traveled from her guts to gush out of her mouth, with a puckering of her lips. And so, over the course of time, Bashira had told her friend about her daily life on the plantation and in the workhouses. Once when their discussions had led them in a random zigzag to talk about the meaning of life, Bashira, with a laugh that seemed to harken back to another time, and full with a current love, told her friend: "One must accept happiness wherever one finds it. You think that your soul or your body will return to the country of our ancestors to find your man, but me, I've come to think that our life is here in this place, and that you and I as well as all the negroes here, we all lost our bet. So, if one can find small moments of pleasure here and there, one must take them." And Aza responded, "You mean grab them fast, like a delicious, sweet orange," trying to untie the heavy knot of pain that lay beneath her friend's words. So, she told her a few stories of raucous children, men with penises that, like bananas boiling in water, would stir as soon as they saw women's bottoms. "Well, they will stiffen as soon as they're in the midst of the action," concluded Bashira, bursting into laughter. And the two women turned toward each other at the same time, with joyful tenderness.

With wear and tear, Bashira had become less talkative, a little absent. The surroundings of her hut still smelled of sweet, tempting odors, but her eyes told a story of fatigue and a farewell soon to come. Bashira's steps were becoming heavy, the movement of her arms were slowing down, and often she sat on her low chair as if her body were asking for mercy. Powerless, Aza would watch her friend who she knew was younger than herself but whose labor in the workhouses had aged her prematurely. Now that she could simply dedicate herself to her garden plot, it seemed that her bones had settled on themselves as if they were getting closer to the earth. When Aza would caress her back, it seemed more fragile, tired, exhausted. *My sister, don't leave me.* When she kissed her, she was afraid of the slight, wispy breath that escaped her lips. The laughter they shared took on a new rhythm: it seemed to halt midway as if it were planting a good-bye kiss. A slight, cold air then pierced Aza's heart. *No, my sister, don't cry.* Silently, with a nod of the head, Bashira stopped the flow of distress that overwhelmed her friend's face. *No, my sister. No.*

Trying to keep a calm face, Aza nevertheless showed the blow to the guts caused by Bashira's collapse. It's as if this new loss to come made her previous losses heavier to bear. She tried to remember Mali's face, the physical traits that the years, despite the burns she had imposed on herself, had inevitably erased from her memory. And these forgettings seemed to her to be a foreboding sign of another good-bye. Good-bye to her life over there, good-bye to the love she carried within that she wore like a dress whose colors were fading; she was sad to have captured a mere impression of happiness, a sensation of a diffuse pleasure that returned only when her despairing spirit conjured it. Sometimes, of course, she would find her man, like a flash of lightning in the pull of Désirée's smile, or a mundane movement of her hands, in the long silhouette of her fluid gestures. But she felt that with the loss of Bashira, it would be like an excavation of a possibly unconquerable ditch, and she'd have nothing but dreams as insipid as a piece of sugarcane so chewed up that only bland saliva remains.

In the drawing room of the big house, Boulet had kept a family portrait in which he could be seen standing with his hands resting on his wife's shoulders, with their two girls both leaning on the armrest of the mother's chair. It was an oil painting in which the people seemed stuck in an uneasy and gauche pose, which made them even more unlikable in Aza's eyes, but each time she wanted to put herself in that painting, changing the entire cast and scene. She'd replace the armchair, now covered in a dark, complex tapestry, with a flowering tree, loose earth under bare feet, instead of the pretentious tapestry. She'd insert an image of herself happy and fulfilled, and one of Mali with his open smile, dazzling with love and desire, then she'd put the portraits of Désirée and Guillaume, the happy accomplices. After meeting Bashira, she added her image, including her in the newly formed group, which would create a perfect family where happiness would mock social conventions.

One day, the planter Boulet found her absorbed in this portrait, so much so that she didn't hear him enter the room. Interpreting this daydreaming as a sign of her attachment to him, he concluded that she must be dreaming of taking Madame Boulet's place. He had already talked to her about divorce, which was still unauthorized in France—even though his wife had already left the premises, under the pretext that the Caribbean climate made their girls ill. Aza, under the name Agathe, took refuge in silence as she listened to Boulet's wild imaginings, his ridiculous gibberish, his sighs leading to the pressure of his hand on the young woman's backside. In September 1792 divorce became legal in France. The planter Boulet learned of it when he received the notice of divorce from his wife, the cause being the husband's years-long absence. It seemed that Madame Boulet wanted to marry her lover as soon as possible, the merchant from Nantes with whom she had formed a couple since her departure from the colony.

Seven years had already passed. According to Boulet, it was becoming harder for the white settlers to wed their domestics. Marriages between whites and the formerly enslaved were rare. Aza no longer believed Boulet's promises of freedom, of emancipation. Despite her doubts, she had chosen the least risky path for her daughter. Désirée was special. At first, Boulet protected her more, even though from time to time he would tell Aza, in a gruff voice, "You should do a better job of looking after your daughter." Over the years, he'd say, "You should talk to Désirée." Then, he'd say, "You should probably keep her close to you. People are often talking about her." "People are afraid of her, both whites and blacks." "Don't let her go out at night." How does anyone prevent Désirée from doing anything? Deep down, Aza felt angry at herself for not finding another way out. But what choice did she have? She had done the best she could for her daughter. She believed that her son Guillaume would take care of his little sister when she was no longer alive. She was also certain of her impending death.

It was a fact that Aza wouldn't withstand much longer. In some way she already felt far from the world. And if Bashira were to pass, how long could she continue to hold on? That would be the last straw. The body has its own laws that we can't always change with tisanes, lotions, herbs, and potions. Her body was slipping slowly toward the earth from whence it came, and she knew that she couldn't hold it back. She had prepared Désirée as best as she could, but Désirée had created her own world and would make fun of other people's worlds.

All around them, change was happening. Ever since she had placed her feet on the ground in Saint-Domingue, she had watched the settlers conspiring against the colonial administration, then against the freemen—while the *ti blancs* banded together. She knew that the war had only just begun and that she couldn't predict how it would end. Now, the former slaves were called cultivators, but shouldn't a farmer have land in order to farm? Some refused to return to the plantations, and a good number of them like Bashira decided to care only for their small plots of land, their place for vegetables. Out of frustration, many of them were getting organized, and no one could blame them. Who knew what was going through the white planters' heads? One couldn't trust them.

She knew about Louverture, this former slave who had fought the Spanish, then the English, then the French. He was general-in-chief, the commander of the island, but would the fate of the cultivators truly change for the better? What would become of all those who, like her, had boarded these ships? From time to time, other vessels would be left stranded, bringing threats of war and decisions from the metropole. These ships were like immense objects that were gorging on the misfortunes of human beings, their holds filled with either human flesh or spices. Sometimes when Aza would stare at the sea, far in the distance, it was as if she could feel the jolts of the large vessel again, hear the noise of the waves, the inaudible growls of anger and fear. She couldn't see the ships without shivering. She couldn't look at the sea without feeling the wave of an old but never painless despair return to haunt her.

I'm telling you to wait, Gilles. Aren't we fine here? It's so sweet feeling the sun's warmth on our bare legs. I don't want to come down from this tree. Not yet. I'm waiting for Zinga to arrive. I know that the three of you want to wash up in the river. We'll go soon. Ma Aza won't be happy if you go home dirty. We'll all go and wash up in the river soon, but I won't move an inch until I see Zinga.

Your Zinga is nice, but he doesn't know my name. He never says it. He sees only you, Désirée, it's not fair. I'm attractive too. He could be my older brother, like Caleb. That way, I'd have two older brothers. And you, Gilles, stop whining.

But it's not fair, I wanted to stay with Ma Aza. Désirée never wants to stay put. She's always on the move.

You don't know what you want, Gilles. Your mother isn't going to come get you if you're always whining like a baby.

Virginie, I keep telling you not to talk about that. Look at the mountains, could you tell them apart from the clouds? They're stunning. It's as if they're stuck together. I'd love to enter the clouds and drown myself in them.

We can't drown in clouds, Désirée. I'm only twelve years old, and I know that. You're older, you should know it.

Yes, Ms. Virginie-know-it-all. Thanks.

She's going to tell us again that her brother taught her to read and write.

Be quiet, Gilles, you don't know anything. You're only five years old. Be quiet. Your mother is the one who won't return. That's what I think anyway.

Oh, that's enough! Be quiet children, you're talking too much. I'm going to tell you a story—one of Ma Aza's stories that you're going to like. But you shouldn't argue like this, that's not good. Ma Aza won't be happy if I tell her that you're bickering all the time. Listen to me carefully. When we look inside ourselves, we see all the world's colors. Let's go! Take my hand. Close your eyes. First, I feel the color blue. It's floating above our heads, it's sprinkling a light rain of soft needles on our skin. It's soft and falls without stopping. Then I feel the color yellow coming. It's warm, juicy, unpredictable, and mocking. Gilles, do you feel it on the tips of your ears and nose? It tickles you. But the green is always there too, I hear the rustling of the leaves and the smell of rain, that's it . . .

Ha ha ha! What are you rambling on about, my poor Désirée? What's this gibberish!?

It's Fatima, she's returned. I'm afraid of her, Désirée. She's mean.

Virginie's right. I'm afraid of her too, Désirée.

And why are you afraid of me? Because I tell the truth. Those colors, I'm going to tell you all about them. Blue is the bright sound made by the machete when it cuts the sugarcane stalk. It's quick, merciless, we don't hear it coming. Yellow is the unfaithful voice of those that strike you in the back to save their own skin, blacks like you, captured Africans like you, rebels like you, freed people, small-time white planters, white riffraff like Ti Griffe. It's the smell of betrayal.

Don't talk about Guillaume, Fatima. He's my brother, and we love each other.

And green is the smell of fear. It's Gilles's fear, he's afraid of everything.

I'm not afraid. I just want my mother, that's all.

Leave him alone, Fatima. He's only five.

And me, I'm old enough to know suffering and rage.

You're sixteen, stop lying.

You'll never understand anything, you idiot. You little snotty-nosed kid.

I forbid you to insult him, Fatima. It's been a while since I've seen you. I thought you had left for good.

Yeah, why don't you go away?

Oh, my dear Virginie, where do you think I should go? Go find your brother in the land of our ancestors? You'd be better off forgetting him. Don't you understand that he's dead just like

Gilles's mother? Stop telling yourself these tall tales! In fact, what would you do without me? I'd rather stay with all of you—ever since Désirée met her friend Zinga, life is not at all boring. We're going to all have fun. He likes to touch Désirée, to tell her sweet nothings.

Désirée, ask her to leave, because Gilles and I don't like her. The three of us are fine without her. Tell her to leave, Désirée.

Zinga watched her sleep in his arms like a child with sighs reaching the depths of his being, which he'd thought he'd left back there, in Africa. Since arriving in the colony, he had slept with a good number of women: tall, strong ones, young ones, the less young ones, black ones, mixed ones, even white ones who would experience pleasure naively, even before he touched them. He was a man who loved women's softness, he liked to give and receive pleasure, without expecting anything more than that, without wanting anything else. Without pretending, without hiding anything. But this woman who had stars in her sad eyes was different, he felt vulnerable in her presence, as if his body's nakedness revealed parts of himself he thought were too buried to show themselves in broad daylight. With her, he learned the language of streams that snake through the land, belonging to no one, he smelled the scent of flowers before the appearance of buds, he heard the screams of children without seeing them. He let her lead him in her world without ever being able to fully enter it. That day, he found her with a desperate look in her eyes, with a child's voice and laughter that rang sometimes bitter and hard; she went from groaning to laughing, and from laughing to moaning. He cradled her in his arms until she calmed down. He had to protect her, that he knew. He knew the enemy on the outside and could deal with him, but he didn't know what to do with the demons that gnawed her from within.

Around them, the world was becoming more and more tumultuous. Since taking his hand and leading him to the riverbank, where he let her bring him when it was raining, when they had both tousled their hair, wet from the water, from the moment they had undressed as they stood facing each other, he had seen her squat to whisper words that he didn't quite understand before lying on her side and inviting him to join her, making them a multicolored rug out of her soaked skirt. When he touched her, he trembled, and felt even more cautious since she refused to have him lay on top of her. The only time he did, her whole body twitched and she jumped up straightaway, with bewildered eyes, gasping for breath. They made love side by side, then she straddled him, and he got lost in her big, sad eyes and her smiling lips.

From that day on, she would dance in his dreams, skipping about under his watchful eye, hopping in each of his steps.

Around them, angry exchanges continued among the whites, the freedmen, and the rebels gathered in the mountains. Zinga the African had joined a group of Congo people even though he had a hard time taking orders. Having become distrustful since they had dragged him on this ship of tragedy, he learned to observe peoples' behavior, never simply trusting what they said. With a suspicious eye, he heard others speak about the important people in the army, from the likes of Louverture to Rigaud, about their actions especially—their power struggles, the war they were waging, one of them in the South, the other one in the West. Zinga was not very surprised to learn that Rigaud, Pétion, and another army chief had left for the metropole at the end of the year. In the meantime, Dessalines had been named commander-in-chief of the Western Army and General Moyse, supposedly a relative of Toussaint, so they said, was named commander-in-chief of the Northern Army. What was behind all these moves? During this time, the former slaves found themselves in the middle of all this, as they were trying to forge a life in which the sun didn't exist solely to indicate the time to start working like mules. Was it too much to ask for? Was it too much to refuse to break one's back and to find oneself silver-haired while working for others? Zinga would often watch the storm take over the eyes of those around him. A sad and wild storm, in both women and men who no longer wanted to be the last ones in line, those who were the first ones standing, the first ones affected, the first ones to fall when conflicts erupted.

While she slept next to him, Désirée seemed very far away from this angry world that was at boiling point, from which he would have liked to save her. And yet sometimes, as if coming from a wounded child, a scream would escape her lips: like a litany cut off from its momentum, the scream would stop suddenly and her whole body would twist as if it were under the influence of an internal whirlwind, which he could do nothing to stop.

PART TWO

These last years had matured him, and he now understood what Ma Aza had told him one day when he was feeling even more confused and out of sorts than usual. "You must be patient, my little Guillaume, you are going to shine like the sun after rainfall. We must wait for it, but its rays slide slowly across the scattering clouds: they arrive at the summit of mountains, and then suddenly, everything becomes clear and luminous. Let time and life take their course, my son."

Guillaume wiped his eyes with his shirtsleeve, and he, ordinarily so calm, so collected, began to pound the ground with enraged and determined feet. The fine dust from the road raised by his boots left a white trail behind him, but Guillaume paid it no mind. He had to find Désirée. He wanted to make sure that she was okay.

Aza passed away quietly that night. The doctor who had been called for help could only confirm her death, mumbling that she had probably died of pneumonia that hadn't been properly treated. Many heads nodded, muttering that they expected this, given Bashira's death two months earlier. Over time, Guillaume had come to view the two women as a unit that formed his defense, even though he knew fully well that they couldn't do much in the face of life's treachery. Knowing that they were there for him, attentive to him no matter where he was—this had given him strength that he now held onto so as not to sink into despair. It had been hard for him to accept the passing of Ma Bashira, who had always protected him from words and actions meant to hurt him. Ma Aza's death now left him feeling like an abandoned child, shaken to the core.

His protective reflex toward Désirée took over for a moment. If this new loss was affecting him so much, Guillaume wondered with growing anxiety how his little sister was doing. He hadn't seen the girl, but the woman who had discovered

Aza's lifeless body told him that Désirée had suddenly slipped out of the hut, probably heading for the hills. The planter Boulet, with his reddened and bloated face, said that he'd make the funeral arrangements and take care of Désirée as he had promised her mother. Yet no one standing near Aza's body believed him.

The young man had returned to the Martineau plantation to take a horse and set off looking for Désirée. Inside, both anger and fear filled his heart, but the sadness of losing Aza remained constant, heavy, relentless—biding its time to strike. He felt it interfering with his thoughts, mixing in with the scents of dawn, a puff of air on the cheek like the hand of the woman who had given him so much. How could he get used to her absence, when knowing that she was merely a few kilometers away had anchored him? Ma Aza. To all the children who were put in her care, she had been a solid rock, a smooth and soft stone where they knew they could lay down the burdens of their day, share their smiles, and simply be themselves without fear of receiving slaps or murderous looks. For him, she was a flowering tree, strong and fragrant, capable of protecting without being menacing, with generous, soothing foliage.

So as not to be overcome with grief, he held on tightly to the anger aroused by the unexpected conversation between Boulet and Martineau, his godfather, even if the latter was being more respectful, less cynical than his neighbor. Still stunned by the sight of Ma Aza's lifeless body, Guillaume was moving forward, on the lookout for Désirée, when he overheard Boulet's voice mention the young woman's name. Quickly yet cautiously, he moved close to the partially opened parlor shutters. ". . . She's half-crazy, this girl. She has a mad look about her." "Don't exaggerate!" Martineau replied. "Désirée is different, it's true, but you can't just throw her out." "No, but I can send her away from here, or find a way to make her calm down." "What are you saying, Boulet? . . . you've watched this girl grow up! You can't just to do whatever." Guillaume quickly moved away from the shutters, edging his way to avoid being seen, more than ever resolved to find his little sister and protect her.

In spite of himself, the previous year, near Limbé, he had helped to capture a young man considered crazy. Such an unfortunate man. A small-time white man, apparently on the lowest rungs of the hierarchy given his untidy clothes, his unkempt hair, and his dirty hands. He was shrieking inarticulately and struggling as he moved his arms and legs. What had led him here? How did he get to this place where he was acting like a trapped animal forsaken by human speech? Guillaume shuddered when he saw four men punch him to control him. They opened his mouth and forced him to swallow a potion. Then they savagely tied him up, and because he was still wriggling, they doused him from head to toe with a pail of cold water. According to what those who had captured him said, he was going to be interned in an asylum that treated people like him: the madmen and madwomen. They had potions to tranquilize him, to lull him to sleep for a long while. When he returned home from Martineau's place and told people about this incident, the cabinetmaker said that they beat them sometimes or locked them up in a darkened room to calm their nerves.

All these stories came back to him today. Did the planter Boulet want to put Désirée away? How could she be locked up in some cell? The one who could never stay still, she who would skip more than walk? She who seemed to be always perched in a treetop? What would happen to her, the young woman who was so sensitive that the pain of a little boy had made her lose her voice for five days?

Guillaume was barely nine years old, which means that Désirée was definitely ten. In the woods nearby, the two children had been playing hide-and-seek, knowing full well that Guillaume would never find Désirée unless she let him. Some unusual sounds had startled them: the stamping of horses, overexcited voices, and children's cries. Hand in hand, they ran toward the Boulet plantation. Little Gilles was screaming. Guillaume didn't know that someone so small could make so much noise. His mouth was wide open, everyone could see his baby teeth, his runny nose, and his two tiny hands reaching for his mother. An unknown man on a brown horse was firmly holding the negress named Rose, whose eyes, brimming with tears, were fixed on her son in silent communication. He was thrashing around while screaming, but a workhouse slave held him in place. Impatient and annoyed, the planter Boulet encouraged the man to leave quickly to cut this scene short. Désirée had screamed, "Where is Ma Aza?" "You know she was supposed to go to town today," Guillaume thought, but the words didn't cross his lips. Everyone had stopped talking, because suddenly Rose began to moan. No words escaped her mouth. She kept looking at her son, and a continuous, piercing sound, coming from a dark and frightening place, escaped her barely half-opened lips. The man tried to gag her with his left hand, but she bit him, and he probably needed to use both hands to keep her seated on the horse. He was satisfied with holding her more tightly against him with his right arm. The sound of her voice continued in an overwhelming monotone, and Guillaume shuddered without knowing why. Désirée rushed at the man and yelled something at him. He pushed her away violently. The manager who was accompanying Boulet motioned to a slave to move the young girl away. Petrified, the two children saw the man gallop away with the negress Rose, but although the dust had long settled, her moans could still be heard. Little Gilles had stopped screaming, he was no longer moving, only tears were falling from his eyes. When Aza returned from town an hour later, she ran to find the planter Boulet, but returned with a closed, hard face, shimmering eyes, and a voice shaking with anger. Boulet had once again lost at gambling, and a certain Sinclair, this planter from Dondon, had claimed three slaves he had chosen himself. He would send for the other two but wanted to leave with Rose that same day. Boulet's hands were tied, otherwise he would've risked losing his plantation. He had given his word, and he couldn't do anything about it. The planter Sinclair hadn't wanted the child, who was too scrawny and sullen. Boulet claimed to have pleaded to keep Rose but wasn't able to change Sinclair's mind. Désirée stamped her feet, overwhelmed her mother with all kinds of protests, and Guillaume pleaded too. "I can't do anything, children," tirelessly repeated Aza, who had taken little Gilles in her arms and was cradling him. She felt a deep affection for this little child whose mother had to wean him very early, under pressure from Boulet. For a long time, Aza shared the pain of the mother and the child, both so bound to each other. She had to show patience and tenderness so that baby Gilles would finally calm down in the mornings. The day the man from Dondon came to take away his mother, Aza rocked him all night, and the following morning and night. He refused to eat, no longer spoke, no longer cried. Already puny, baby Gilles died three weeks later. The planter Boulet said that he wouldn't tell the mother, but she found out anyway. News came from Dondon that she had hanged herself. A few days later, Sinclair who was furious and vindictive, came to protest to the planter Boulet. Apparently, he wanted Boulet to give him another female slave to replace the negress Rose. For several days, a morose atmosphere reigned over Aza's hut and over the children under her charge. All the mothers who came to get their children at the end of the day spoke about Rose's departure, the death of baby Gilles, and Boulet's wickedness. At the market the following Sunday, everyone was talking about it, condemning Boulet and his bad behavior. "He's losing more than he's getting, but he persists." "Now his bad luck will grow, he has Rose and her son's blood on his hands. Misfortune will follow him to his grave." "I never liked this guy. His smile is as fake as a summer wind promising rain." "They will come to haunt him at night, I swear!" At Martineau's plantation, this was also a popular topic of conversation for several days. "Boulet should have insisted that the child be sold with his mother. It makes more sense. Now, we have a double loss." "It's true that Boulet did have to feed the little one, but in a few years the child could have begun to do small jobs. Now, he's lost everything." Meanwhile, the differing perspectives agreed on the fact of the disastrous consequences of Boulet's evil ways. "His wife left because of that. Each time, he promises to stop, and he keeps doing it . . . He's going to end up losing his plantation."

Thinking about it after all these years, Guillaume tells himself ironically that without a doubt this tragedy could have been avoided, since in August of the same year the civil commissioners Sonthonax and Polvérel proclaimed equality and liberty for all slaves. But could history be rewritten?

Guillaume was the first to realize that Désirée had not said a single word since the death of baby Gilles. Not one word. She didn't say "Good morning," she didn't talk about the rainbow she saw the day before, she didn't say that the birds were complaining about the winds' squalls, nor did she mention looking for a new piece of cloth to add to her collection of multicolored fabric. She didn't announce, while laughing, that she'd go hide so Guillaume could come and find her again and again. Nor did she say how Bashira's jams smelled like the sun, even at night. No, she no longer said "Good morning, little brother." She no longer hummed to herself. It was total silence in the early morning, at high noon, at night. Désirée's voice was missing. Panicked, Guillaume tried to draw Ma Aza's attention, but the mother–wet nurse was fighting against her helpless anger, her immense grief, and would just check Désirée's temperature. She made her herbal tea, and would bathe all the children with leaves of verbena and soursop to calm them and ease them into sleep. Désirée remained silent for five days. Aza, now worried, wanted to send for a healer, when her daughter began to speak again as if nothing had changed. At least no one noticed right away. She simply began to murmur, to laugh, and to talk to herself.

Baby Gilles's death left its mark on all of them, but it shattered Désirée's spirit, which Guillaume knew and had always known. For him, too, certain events had changed the way he saw the world, how he moved in the world, how he approached it. Not in a fiery way like Désirée, but gradually, like an accumulation of facts, situations, sensations, and emotions that had taken root in him, mixing together, making their way, coming up against each other, and creating a coherent whole that was him. As his mother Aza had predicted, he had become a man. He got to know fear when he ran to meet Aza on the night of the insurrection. His indignation shone brightly in his eyes when he heard jeers that relegated him to a separate world, an inferior world: "Unscrupulous little griffe." He felt anger after these insults, whispered in fear of the planter Martineau's reaction, but insults nonetheless: "Little bloodsucking whitey." But the most heartbreaking one was when a voice yelled, "Motherless good-for-nothing." He had cried bitterly and felt even worse for having pushed Aza away when she wanted to console him—so ashamed when he saw pain clouding her eyes. More recently, his grandfather's departure for the East confirmed the fact that he'd changed, he was better prepared to take life's blows. The year before, right after the attack on Au Cap by Admiral Villaret de Joyeuse, Jean-Claude Gillot had left. He no longer wanted to fall prey to interracial massacres like the ones that had followed the attempted takeover of the city. "Blood will be shed, it won't be mine," he declared before leaving, without thinking to say good-bye to his grandson. It was the planter Martineau, embarrassed, who told Guillaume at nightfall. Guillaume had taken in the news with an indifference that had not surprised him, but since then a diffused anger spread in him; his anger wasn't against this man who had always held him in contempt, but against this society that was based on injustice, exploitation, and disrespect for human beings. Martineau's decision to leave for France at the end of the month didn't surprise him either. Guillaume wasn't angry at Martineau for attending to his own problems and for fleeing this land that had made him rich, while the society was falling apart right before his eyes. According to the steward and the surgeon, Martineau, unlike others, always behaved appropriately toward those who worked with him. He saw to it that his negroes weren't tortured or hit unjustly. Yet Guillaume wondered whether one could talk about justice in such a barbarous system. When he thought about Bashira's decline at the end of her life, he would become consumed by indignation and anger. But he also knew that other planters had been excessively cruel. What must seem petty to him, who had never been enslaved, must have made a real difference in the lives of the men and women who worked on the sugar and coffee plantations. These men and women who now fought to keep their basic rights: freedom, land ownership, and wages for their work. Guillaume, who was always rather calm, felt the need to fight the itching of his hands and the tugging at his heart.

His friend Florent Manigat, a free black man, a captain in the colonial army who had since left to join the Indigenous Army, had told him about the major moments in the siege of

Crête-à-Pierrot. With a feeling so palpable that Guillaume was himself filled with pride, Florent had described for him the brazen acts of courageous contact, not only from the soldiers and officers but also the cultivators in the region. Risking death, they had lured the French in front of the small fort, then disappeared in the trenches surrounding the walls. Of course, some perished in doing this, but they caused the death of several French soldiers who fell under fire coming from the fort. Florent wouldn't stop talking about the two people who had made an impression on him. "You know, Guillaume, even amid the sound of weapons, you realize what's essential. You see it and you hold on to it so you can return to it later. She would wear men's clothing, but I knew immediately that it was a woman. Strands of hair escaped from her cap. She moved so swiftly that my eyes had a hard time following her. She brought munitions to the men, she shouted orders, she would encourage others, hurl abuses, and didn't hesitate to use the rifle slung across her shoulder. Sweat beaded her face and she wiped it away impatiently with her hand. She was so brave and beautiful that I wanted to embrace her. I learned her name: Marie-Jeanne." Florent told the story of how, after several attempts, the mulatto Lamartinière, Marie-Jeanne's companion, incredibly courageous himself, managed to get three hundred men to exit the fort. Hundreds of French soldiers died during this operation. But the second occasion that had greatly impressed Florent was hearing Dessalines speak. Before leaving the fort, the general-in-chief spoke to the troops to motivate them, and he confirmed that he wouldn't stop until victory. "If Dessalines surrenders to them a hundred times, he will betray them a hundred times." Florent had repeated these words so often that they came back to Guillaume when Dessalines surrendered to the French a few weeks later. Like so many others, he had followed the deeds of the black generals: Christophe, Pétion, Clerveaux, and Dessalines in particular. He had questioned some of them, had felt completely betrayed by others, for example, the measures taken against the cultivators, even though it was under Toussaint's orders. The execution of Charles and Sanite Belair had also demoralized him, like an absurd and cruel double loss. But he wasn't overly surprised when Dessalines rallied the insurrectionists after the secret meeting in Arcahaie because Dessalines's words remained engraved in his memory: "If Dessalines surrenders to them a hundred times, he will betray them a hundred times." "You know," Florent added, "when you hear that man speak, you feel deep within you that he sees beyond what you can see with your own eyes. I can't explain it, Guillaume, but after having listened to him, you look around you and you see a country."

When it was his turn, Guillaume joined the Indigenous Army and felt a sense of deep satisfaction—a mixture of serenity and contentment. Like on that day in childhood when the words "Motherless good-for-nothing" resonated within him with less force than before, he returned to Aza with eyes still red and sad. She opened her arms to him. "Mother," he said as if it were a question, a call, an offering. She had smiled at him, embracing him too, whispering, "My son."

He would always be grateful to Martineau for having convinced Boulet to let Aza take care of him. Otherwise, what would have happened to him? As a scrawny newborn, weak and orphaned, without Aza's care, he probably would not have survived. And most of all, without Bashira and Aza, what kind of man would he have become? Aza fed him, he drank her breast milk like Désirée his milk sister, but he also felt that he was Bashira's son. There are so many ways to give life to a human being. As someone who grew up without a father, how lucky he felt to have two mothers!

As he thought he would, Guillaume found Désirée at the stream's edge where she loved to dip her toes. Crouched on the rocks, she balanced her body from right to left, then from front to back without stopping. Guillaume placed one hand on her arm, and she nestled against him.

"Little brother, she's gone. I'm in pain and the children are scared."

"I know, I know. But you can't stay here."

Guillaume knew that he had to take the young woman away, but he hadn't yet decided where to take her. His friends had enlisted in the army like himself; if she went to Martineau's plantation, he couldn't protect her from Boulet—the two planters were too close. Moreover, Martineau, who was getting ready to leave, was negotiating the sale of the plantation, so there were many visitors coming and going in the space. In fact, no one knew what would become of the French planters' plantations—they wouldn't be ideal hiding places given the current circumstances. He was thinking about where to go when suddenly Désirée leaped up and began jumping up and down.

"I know where we could hide. She told me to call on her if I was ever in trouble. She'll help us."

"Who is it, little sister? Who are you talking about?"

"You'll see, follow me."

Jérôme thought of nothing but this woman. He had eyes only for her. He had spoken to her two or three times, and she had smiled automatically, answering him with a friendly but cautious expression. This Saturday would mark thirty-two days since he'd seen her for the first time. He was with his family, who were visiting his father's planter friends, the Lavilles, who had a good number of people of color and free blacks in their social circle. She was a poised young woman, with a modulated voice, dressed in expensive finery from head to toe. That was Jeanne Mercier.

He knew immediately that she came from a wealthy family, a family of black landowners who had large plantations in the South of the country. People also said that her uncle and two of her brothers were officers in the French Army. They had undoubtedly become richer than his own father, who had had trouble ever since this famous war between France and England which had lasted for seven years. The planter Beauvais had never completely recovered financially. Luckily, Sophie married well, and Julien had already found a position as a public servant in Paris. At any rate, he never had the intention to return to settle down in Saint-Domingue. More and more, Jérôme felt the paternal pressure on him, the mulatto son. Technically, the young man wouldn't have trouble continuing in his father's footsteps. He was intelligent enough to make the right decisions, he wouldn't take pointless risks and would slowly but surely continue to expand the family business. But the political situation was becoming more and more difficult. How could he even imagine maintaining a plantation in such a contentious climate? He hated problems of all kinds and feared the looming financial setbacks. Fighting to get the plantation back on track was out of the question amid uprisings, unending revolts, armed conflicts, or the aftermath of conflicts. Agitated and nervous as the situation in the colony worsened, Jérôme almost resented his father for not leaving it all behind and choosing instead to stay put while so many of his friends had left. Yet Jérôme knew very well that it was his mother who refused to leave.

Upon returning home after the Lavilles' reception, his father let it be known that Mercier's daughter would be an excellent match for Jérôme—a comment that Jérôme quickly understood. Once, the conversation between his father and some of his white friends had turned to the subject of marriage and family alliances. Someone mentioned the case of a white planter whose profits were taking a turn for the worse and who married a woman of color, who had just received an inheritance from her family. She was an educated woman, much more so than her husband. The marriage had taken place and the union had borne fruit. Not only were children born, but this white man had now become one of the most important planters of the region. Then an adolescent, Jérôme had questioned his father privately: "But what does the woman and her family get? She just married a boor without a dime to his name." "She and her family gained in terms of social status. Don't forget that discrimination against people of color is still strong. With this marriage, they gain a less dark shade of skin and her children are now considered quadroons." Usually, the planter never discussed matters of skin color in front of Mathilde unless she raised the question herself. On that day, the appearance of his mother had put an end to the conversation, but Jérôme understood what his father had not said: a young black woman, even a rich and cultured one, who married a mulatto would also be better off.

Thus they came back to this distinction based on skin color. Mulattoes shared common interests with whites, and Jérôme didn't understand why whites flaunted skin color to keep mulattoes in a subordinate position. He'd read excerpts from *Mémoire en faveur des gens de couleur ou sang mêlés de Saint-Domingiue et des autres îles françaises de l'Amérique*. To see disgraceful ideas written had upset him. It felt like he had gotten smaller in the wake of all these kinds of bans which targeted mulattoes. He remembered a sentence that seemed to summarize the condition of mulattoes in St. Domingue. "Contempt is only one step away from injustice. And the mulatto must be right ten times for justice to happen only once." It was clear that they were judged this way because of the color of their skin.

Shy and withdrawn, he had dared to offer this opinion for the first time a few months ago, during a party that included the Lespinasse couple and their daughter Cécile, who was known for her daring opinions. Living up to her reputation, she answered ironically that the question of color was a pretext for keeping the black slaves in their inhumane situation, and that it was contradictory not to use the same reasoning for all groups. Facing all the eyes awaiting his answer, Jérôme stammered an incomprehensible response before moving away, with a glass of wine in hand.

Even more put out by her response, which he thought was cowardly, he brought up the question with his mulatto friends, who came out with their usual arguments, as he expected. First, the census of 1782 had identified two groups within the population of people of color: those who had European blood coursing through their veins, and those who didn't have any. Those who were called "free blacks" were part of this second group.

"This Cécile must be really angry with the mulattoes because even though her family is wealthy, they will never be our equal!"

"They no doubt have slaves too, and they're really harsh with them."

"You should have asked her if all the free blacks are as wealthy as she is. And what about those who work like slaves to survive? That's what you call freedom!"

During a stroll in Haut-Limbé, very far from the town, Jérôme had met an elderly couple who worked the land. The man had told him with pride that they were free, having obtained their freedom after having worked on a sugar plantation in Limbé. "Freedmen from the savannah," that's what they were called, his father said. Poor people who worked a small parcel of land to meet their basic needs.

Jérôme told himself that in theory they were all free because there were no longer any slaves in Saint-Domingue. Some blacks worked on the few plantations still standing. Some grew vegetables, root vegetables, all kinds of produce that they'd sell in the market on plots they owned, or rather plots they'd claimed after the uprising. Others were fighting in the hills, either the rebels or the bandits, as the whites called them. In fact, the true battles took place on the ground, while he and his friends were having discussions in salons. Some mulattoes had joined the troops. At times, he also thought of enlisting, but which troop would he choose? Those fighting for France or those fighting against France? He learned that during the combat at Fort de la Crête-à-Pierrot in March of last year, the mulatto Lamartinière had fought alongside the rebels. Of course, this same Lamartinière was going to enlist in the French Army after the surrender, like many of the black and mulatto officers. This same colonial army would chase rebels. The situation would change from one day to the next, and Jérôme could no longer make sense of any of it sometimes. In such a context, how does one trust anyone? Could one trust the white officers? But the idea of the island of Saint-Domingue in the hands of the rebels scared him even more. What destiny would they have in store for people of color?

Jérôme wondered what the beautiful Jeanne thought of this difficult and complex situation. Was she tired of racking her brains over these questions? Honestly, he didn't think she would remember him. She didn't seem particularly interested in his attempts to start a conversation that was neither trite nor pretentious. She and her friends were chatting and paid him little mind. He had felt rather stupid, small, insignificant, and invisible. "You must show more confidence in your moves," Sophie and Julien would repeatedly tell him—both of whom were lucky to have inherited an innate arrogance from their father. In addition, Sophie was lucky to have inherited an inner grace from their grandmothers. Mathilde came from Sénégal, and she was tall, beautiful, and strong and remained that way despite the wear and tear on her body and despite the indignation of her status, which remained degrading in spite of her union with the planter Beauvais. She seemed to keep a sense of dignity that made her almost unreachable, to Jérôme's eyes. He'd tell himself sometimes that the two oldest had gotten all the admirable traits from their parents, and that at his birth only random traits, a personality prone to a perpetual search for approval and a sorrowful absence of talent, remained. In fact, as his father had implicitly suggested, it would be good for him to marry a free black woman whose wealthy family could help him build capital. What would his more radical friends say? Those friends who considered the free blacks, who called themselves Creoles, the true children of this land, to be their worst enemies?

Marrying this young woman, a free black woman from a wealthy family, would in fact be the solution to a great number of problems. Is that why I think so often of her? Am I really attracted to her or do I merely see her as an easy and rather pleasant solution to my discomfort? Jérôme sometimes thought this union was like an exit door toward which he must rush without delay, and at other times, he thought it was an illusion that was retreating with the passage of time. He imagined her young and firm body, her bottom swinging beneath her dress, without showing off, only as evidence of pleasure to be shared, and he sighed.

I had slipped a knife into the satchel that I slung across my shoulder. I kept the baton in the camp because I only took it when I went on patrol. The situation had worsened and some thought that it was about to come to a head. I didn't know what lay ahead of me, but I was ready to fight ferociously for my freedom. The cultivators, women and men, joined the fight as well, becoming more and more wary of the French. Like me, they especially didn't want to go back to living under the control of a white man, a black man, a mulatto, or anyone else wanting to enslave them again. Our generals were fighting each other, changing sides as easily as someone changes shirts, while the French had sent for a legion of soldiers to fight them.

A legion of men ready for anything were sent by Napoleon to restore slavery. A total of 35,000 men. Abdoul, the negro from Bayi, had infiltrated a French brigade; he spent a good amount of time describing their weapons, their bayonets, their hats. He had seemed fascinated by their bearing, their age, because it seemed that there were some very young men among them. Abdoul said that some of them had very low morale and complained constantly. Low morale or not, I knew they were more armed than us and that they'd have no pity. Anyway, the battle was tough for them and for us. Many of us lost our lives. We had killed a great number of them too. And what's more, yellow fever was killing them like flies, or the sun on the island would finish them off. The sun here is not a weak one, it can make dizzy even the ones who greet it every day upon waking. Moreover, it seemed that Leclerc had to order fabric to make special hats for men. Round top hats and shirts also to replace the completely torn uniforms. I had a hard time imagining these men coming from so far away, fighting so fiercely for this land that France wanted to keep at all costs. Would these men have come under these conditions unless they'd been forced to do so? Dofi, a young African from our regiment who was always sullen, had remarked: "But some of us are also fighting for this land of Saint-Domingue that we barely know."

"We're not fighting for Saint-Domingue," Moussa answered, "we're fighting for the right to be free." I told myself that what Moussa says is true, but you're not free in empty space, you're free somewhere, and I was attached to this small piece of land covered in mountains. I was attached to the late-night stars at the end of the year that seemed so close that I imagined my breath reaching them in the sky. I was attached to the cool, morning breeze that tickles my eyelids and makes me smile before opening my eyes. I was attached to the smell of the sea that sometimes, suddenly, brushed against my nostrils to remind me that it wasn't so far away. Yes, I wanted to be free here, not in some unknown place. I was tired of all this emptiness all around me. I wanted something real, concrete, like the ground on which I could place my feet, a place that would be mine.

I wasn't afraid to die. I thought of death the way I thought about showers during the rainy season. They can come at any moment, even when we're a little surprised when water trickles from the sky. For some, the first drops always occasion a reflex to retreat. I wasn't afraid of death: it was the season of death after all. War shows no mercy, but no one could have predicted there there'd be so many victims. I'd seen so many comrades return wounded and maimed. I'd seen so many dead. My friend Basir hadn't survived his wounds from the last skirmish. He died in my arms. I wondered how many more like him would die. Would we be victorious? And sometimes I said "we" without knowing whom to include in this group.

I had heard about Toussaint, but couldn't think about it too much. Life continued, or rather the fight was continuing and we had to face it. Dessalines had finally taken command and according to what I was hearing all around me, he was going to the very end. At any rate, with or without officers and generals, blacks would go to the very end. When we've gotten so far, we can't go back; our feet could only move forward on the road even if it was strewn with traps and disappointments. Even if the smell of death invaded our nostrils. No one would want to turn back.

I was in the encampment when I heard the signal: a cry composed of three short, high, and spaced-out notes that I had taught Désirée. She repeated it as we had agreed. She must have a problem; she wouldn't have called otherwise. That's why I was rushing. I hadn't told the others, but they knew they could count on me to show up when needed. We had our rallying cry. But for now, I had to get to the mimosa tree that Désirée and I had chosen as a meeting point. She took a while before choosing this tree because she said the tree had the shape of a woman with open arms. What could have happened to her, the little one?

First, I saw a shadow under the tree, but as a precaution I didn't call out. Luckily because a second later, I saw another one, a male shadow. Who had she come with?

I studied them from afar. There was no question of approaching without knowing who was with her. Would she have come with a friend? Désirée would smile at all of us, humming. But, did she have friends? Most people were afraid of her. I heard that she had a man. Was he with her now? I came closer, quietly. I moved without making noise, or rather making the same noise that leaves make, or the squeaking of a rat. Taking on the color of the long-beaked ani, I camouflaged myself in the landscape. I learned all of this because my survival and that of my companions depended on it. I did it without even realizing it, and in this moment I became acutely vigilant. I fingered the knife in my satchel. I had already gauged the size of the man, in case I had to fight, and decided that I would hit him in the gut.

Suddenly I recognized the face. How crazy to bring a *ti blanc* to this meeting place! I had gotten information on all the people close to her when I met little Désirée for the first time. I knew the story of the little boy who had become an orphan a few days after his birth. I knew about how Aza had fed him, how she took care of him, how the child adored Désirée, and how now as an adult he protected her.

I had found the story of this young boy, half griffe, half white, shocking and amusing, especially when the Martineau plantation's coachman described him to me. Hair the color of a deeply golden ear of corn, his face was mottled with freckles, a slightly puny body, with bowed legs, always following behind Désirée like a small duckling on clumsy feet following its mother—except that the mother duck was long, black, elegant, and whimsical with her wings often spread.

I didn't trust *ti blancs*, in fact I didn't trust the others either: the mulattoes, the blacks who called themselves free blacks, the whites, whom we knew were the enemy, but the others shifted allegiance and could strike you when you least expected. I didn't forget what had happened to Toussaint. But the *ti blancs*, they went everywhere. The *grands blancs* and some mulattoes, the French who came from the metropole, the ones who lived here on the island, everyone used the *ti blancs* when needed. They could be violent and mean, and I understood them. We all had the right to self-defense, but I wouldn't want to be unarmed if we crossed paths. In any case, I couldn't trust this man right away. A strange mix: griffe and *ti blanc!* I had heard of Romaine the Prophetess who had managed to gather a large number of slaves and establish a military encampment, right after the big insurrection in the Léogâne and Jacmel regions. Apparently, he was a griffe too, like Désirée's *ti griffe*. I'd find out what he had to say, this bow-legged *ti griffe*. A point in his favor was that he was very devoted to Désirée and she trusted him. She wouldn't have brought him here otherwise. Beneath her whimsical air, little Désirée had an acute sense of danger.

Something had probably happened to Aza, that was the only explanation that came to mind. But why did the little one feel threatened? Why bring this man here?

It had been six days since he'd seen her. While walking with his comrades in arms, Zinga relived each moment spent with Désirée, as if reliving them in his head helped him to understand her better. He was still feeling her long, strong legs wrapped around his hips, her hands light and soft on his body, her fresh and impulsive laughter music to his ears, her soft bottom in the palm of his hands, her teasing and feverish lips on his skin. After making love, she sat up suddenly, adjusted her long, multicolored skirt, and leaped up, running almost all the way to the river. He heard her humming as if she had already forgotten him, or even worse, she was whispering words he didn't understand. Sometimes, he thought he overheard other voices, but when he turned around, she was always alone.

This wore on his spirit, he who had wanted to remain indifferent and who wanted to have a good time with this young woman who was open, fascinating, and full of life. Without committing, without feeling her need for something more than sexual relations, he was fulfilled. Each time, it was as if he came from far away, then was reborn. She had taken him out of the kind of awakened torpor that put him in a bad mood, as if he were looking at himself from a distance without being able to be either happy or unhappy. He had thought of continuing in this way, but since meeting Désirée he realized that he had been languishing, and that this freedom, which he so cherished, wasn't much use to him.

Zinga had been the leader of Fatir's regiment since his death. Despite his reluctance, he'd ended up giving in to his companions' demands and accepting the responsibility to lead them. He tried to learn as much as possible about what was happening around him before charging ahead. This way, he'd gather information from all sources on the comings and goings of the black generals. He'd long understood that the military chiefs distanced themselves from their followers. Louverture was obsessed with a certain image of Saint-Domingue, a splendid and majestic one, but he had forgotten that it was the sweat of the former slaves that had raised him to his rank. In fact, Louverture had wanted the ancien régime, but with new masters. The cultivators had to either stay on their former plantations or survive in the hills—miserably, fighting for food, for some well-being. Despite his intelligence, Louverture hadn't understood everything. Zinga had seen some former rebels who had reclaimed the plantations. He had seen people bent over, with hoes in hand and sweat running down their sides, their eyes disillusioned once again. Doubt, sadness, and indignation came over men and women. He wasn't surprised when all this anger gathered to set a blazing fire. The uprising against Toussaint Louverture was like a fury, waves originating in Dondon, in Plaisance, in La Plaine du Nord, in Acul, Limbé, and Port Margot—waves against which the old man could do nothing. Three hundred white planters had been killed. General Moyse was right to ask for the land to be divided, since the former slaves couldn't afford big plots after having worn themselves out on this land to make France wealthy. At the same time, Louverture allowed the former planters to return, as if he wanted to reinstate the ancien régime. Moyse had the courage to stand up to him and to side with the cultivators, yet Toussaint ordered the execution of this young man who was even from his own tribe. Rumor was that he had adopted this young man as a nephew. He was executed along with dozens of leaders, men who had fought against slavery, men like Joseph Flaville, who had fought to organize the uprising of 1791. How could Toussaint order the execution of these men? Zinga wondered whether his nomination as governor-for-life and his right to choose his successor had led him to these insane actions. He had wanted to eliminate all his adversaries, as if he alone knew what was in the best interest of Saint-Domingue. And he fell victim to his own strategy.

And even after all the measures taken against the cultivators, all the schemes against the military chiefs, against the rebel chiefs, either with or against France, he'd let himself be captured the year before by the French. Taken on a ship headed for France, with his spouse, other relatives, and his servants. Zinga had heard rumors among comrades in the Indigenous Army, and despite himself, he felt struck by the sad irony of this man's fate. What a destiny! Arriving by ship, fighting for so many years, to then again be forcibly taken onto a ship and then imprisoned in a fort where apparently it was so cold that even those who had been to France and seen snow felt sorry for old Toussaint.

Among the insurgents, news of Louverture's capture had spread, generating a swarm of rebellious actions. Zinga and the other African leaders were organizing even more than before, receiving new recruits at the rate of the increased determination of the disillusioned cultivators. Zinga wondered how the generals could still accept being part of the French troops after the arrival of General Leclerc's expedition, after the capture and arrest of Toussaint Louverture.

At the port, Zinga had seen Rochambeau disembark with his dogs, "the assassins" as they were called. Hounds with mouths full of slobber, they came from the coast of Cuba and were trained to chase negroes. He had seen men torn to pieces by the bulldogs under the public's eye. One woman had fainted, another one with angry eyes had yelled in satisfaction while the dogs were pursuing the runaways, attacking both men and women, barking, their fangs red with blood. The French forces never backed down in their fight against the rebels. Corpses were thrown in the sea, others were burned, some people who were still alive writhed in pain under the fire's onslaught. He had seen faces aflame, chopped body parts jumping as if still attached to living bodies.

So when were the black generals going to decide to join the wave that was rising throughout the entire colony? News came from the South, clearly showing that it would be difficult to stem this tide. Zinga compared what was happening to the unleashed ocean when it made humans understand that they were powerless in the face of the enormous breaking waves, that the sea could take them down in stormy, rapid succession, which they could do nothing to stop.

Zinga sighed. In the end, it would have been better for him to have remained lethargic, suspended, and not involved in the history of this mountainous land. He would have wanted to hold onto the memories of the great plains and let himself be overtaken by images from long ago. But he couldn't hold onto the illusion; the memories were blurring with time. Because it was truly this mountainous land that he treaded day in, day out, and he couldn't pretend to only live in his head. Is that what the mysterious Désirée was doing? Had she retreated in a bubble? Had she decided to live this way so she wouldn't become submerged? She didn't talk much about herself except to share her love of colors, her passion for the waters, the river, the sea, the animals, and the trees.

Was it necessary to take refuge in a universe of mysteries and shadows where the source of power was elsewhere, from the water or the sky, from their God or *lwa* and spirits from Guinea? One Sunday, peering through the church's shutters, Zinga saw the priest brandish his small white wafer as the congregation bowed its head with fervor. Under the negroes' arbor one evening he had seen men and women prostrate themselves, bending not to work but to make offerings of their adoration, faith, and belief to invisible beings, in exchange for a little hope, for even an invisible hand on the shoulder, for a voice murmuring, "You're not alone." He had seen them sing their fear, their hope, their anger, their pain.

When Boukman died, Zinga had just arrived at the camp. He knew no one, he had just escaped from the hut where they put the newly arrived slaves so they could adapt to the weather and the chains. It wasn't like him to chatter, but once he reached the island, words hardly passed his lips. The atmosphere was highly charged, for bands of rebels had just learned of the death of this fierce man who had rejected slavery and who had organized the big ceremony. Zinga remembered that the old negress Joséphine had told him about whites forcing negroes to watch Makandal burn. They had also caught Boukman, and had decapitated him and paraded his head, saying, "The head of Boukman, chief of the rebels." Zinga figured this was undoubtedly meant to frighten negroes. Instead, Boukman's assassination had caused a wave of protest and anger in the rebels' camps. The chiefs gave instructions and wanted to organize solemn services. The rebels yelled even louder with rage; some wanted to leave immediately and burn all the whites, force them to eat their own flesh, and throw them in the sea. Zinga watched the scene in silence, without moving. Suddenly, the atmosphere changed. A big, loud roar of laughter went off, then another, then another one followed. A drum was heard sounding a muffled sound, then louder, and then even louder. Songs burst forth here and there. People started dancing the calenda. Bodies were growing restless, following or taking turns setting the rhythm: singing, dancing to pay respect to the great combatant, to pay respect to life, to say that the fight would continue. Zinga couldn't fully speak the language, yet he had understood.

Since then, he had attended a number of religious ceremonies. He had attended from afar, not convinced that these experiences mattered. But who was he to tell others how to escape from the despair that traveled in their heads and sullied their dreams? Each person was free to decide how to keep it at bay, if only for an instant. He looked from afar and observed the gestures that often seemed inconsistent, mysterious to him. He'd listen to the words: the songs, the incantations—*Omiba, Omiba, you've brought me here, you've told me nothing; you've left me alone with them, you've left me alone, me against them. Where are you? Omiba, Omiba. You've led me here, but you've told me nothing; you've left me alone with them, alone against them. Where are you? Omiba, Omiba.* Men and women lay face down on the ground, raising their eyes to the sky. The drums were playing, laughter burst forth. Everything became sharper: screams, tears, jerky movements, eyes rolled upward, slaughtered animals, bloodshed, burning candles, fires, knives, faces filled with a somber vividness that fascinated Zinga in spite of himself, and finally, compelled to watch and listen, he saw women and men full of an energy increased tenfold, whose steps followed the same pattern, as if an unknown dance instructor had choreographed the steps and a choir director was conducting the singing. He knew he was witnessing the roots of the alliance. He saw men and women who were holding hands, and whose voices reflected each other, and whose faces were animated with the same fervor. Zinga didn't always understand what he heard, but he saw the pain and humiliation transform; he saw the eyes light up; he saw the bent backs stir, full of dignity and zeal; he saw their actions harmonize. Dazzled despite himself, he knew he was seeing the beginnings of the battle.

Cécile quickly closed her fingers over the piece of paper that the servant had slipped her. It was important that her mother not notice it. Even if Esther Lespinasse wouldn't necessarily object to her daughter's actions, she would tell her father, out of loyalty, based on the idea that a wife must share everything with her husband, owing him respect and obedience, and ensuring that the children would submit to their father's authority. Instinctively, she also wanted to protect her daughter from any danger. Cécile had understood that well. But she couldn't remain like that, with arms crossed while around her the world was shifting. Saint-Domingue, the city of Au Cap, the region was changing, the mentality was no longer the same. She knew what was happening in Paris, she read the newspapers. She was following the events in the island's southern region, the fighting that was happening in the country's mountains, she couldn't agree not to lift a finger while the world around her seemed to be moving at an extraordinary speed.

Angeline, whose two brothers had rejoined the Indigenous Army, had put her in touch with a group of free blacks from Au Cap who had joined their ranks. Since learning that more than a thousand blacks had been drowned under Rochambeau's orders, indignation and anger festered in Cécile. How could one even imagine this expedition of extermination led by the French Army, under the orders of Leclerc, and then under his brother-in-law Rochambeau? If she believed the information she'd received, the latter was bloodthirsty, hankering for violence, ready to eliminate all blacks. In whose name? In the service of what cause? Beholden to the France of Voltaire, whose *Treatise on Tolerance* she'd read, to the France of Racine, whose verses she repeated to herself, Cécile didn't know how to connect these cruel acts to the ideas and images that had indeed nourished her. The rebel leaders discussed the language of extermination that the French used shamelessly, without an ounce of remorse. When they crucified a rebel, they called it "raising in dignity." When they had more than one person drowned, whether it was ten people or three hundred, they talked about "trawling." But what saddened and angered the young woman even more was the expression "step into the arena," which is what they used when their bulldogs devoured human beings. Was it fear that drove this type of atrocity? Or was it a feeling of hatred so strong that it sullied any semblance of humanity? Cécile had surpassed the stage of trying to understand, to explain, to analyze. She wanted to act.

Cécile had learned that, in concert with the actions led by the officers and important generals, acts of insurrection and revolt had been organized all over the territory. In the South, the chief rebels were very active. The movement leaving from Corail had succeeded in rallying to its cause a large number of cultivators who were fleeing the plantations when they didn't burn them down along with the sugarcane fields. The same rebel chiefs who had led the maroons from Platon, such as Goman, Nicolas Régnier, Gilles Béneck, also called Ti Malice, were becoming leaders of this new movement. But in fact, wasn't what was happening now the logical conclusion to events connected to the emancipation of the slaves about ten years earlier? Not only did Cécile understand the reactions of the former slaves in connection to the land, but she also shared their frustrations and anger. Of course, they wanted to own it, this land that they had worked to the benefit of those who had enriched themselves. The land for which they had been tortured, mistreated. Now that they were supposedly free, did they have to work like before, with no personal satisfaction? The information that Cécile gathered infuriated her, but also filled her with pride. There was so much courage in these men and women ready for anything to protect their freedom—and despite the torture and the horrible conditions in which their friends died. It seemed that the captured blacks and mulattoes had been thrown in the ships' holds, where sulfur was burned to asphyxiate them. Then their corpses were simply tossed into the sea. But this didn't stop the determination of the rebels, both men and women, despite an order to execute or shoot anyone who was caught as a warning to the others. News of the retaliation spread across the colony, but only reinforced the rebels' will to fight.

Yes, the arrival of the expedition and the rumors of the eventual reinstatement of slavery resulted in stirring up revolt. It was a declaration of war.

Cécile couldn't listen to the stories of this brutality without being horrified. Atrocities had occurred in the rebels' camp as well. Violence was spreading wantonly. It would be naive to think that one could fight without incurring the loss of human life, and the young woman wondered if with each story, with each new horror, she too wasn't losing some of her humanity. But one question returned often to gnaw at her: wasn't slavery the most atrocious crime against humanity? What crime could be crueler than slavery?

Ever since she decided to play a more active role in the struggle, Cécile wrote in her journal daily to release her feelings. She had to be careful and to stop sharing her opinions publicly. She remembered how the planter Beauvais's mulatto son had almost come apart under her very eyes when she showed him the absurdity of his position—or at least that was her hope. He didn't seem to be a bad guy, but his background shaped his ideas. He spent the evening eyeing Mercier's daughter without noticing that everyone knew about his little game. For now, he was spending time with braggart mulattoes who were blind to change. But she thought there'd be many people who were going to have to take a stand in the months to come. The situation was becoming clearer, the struggle was intensifying. She was afraid, but she wouldn't have been able to look at herself in the mirror if she weren't doing something. In fact, her role was simple: listen to what was being discussed at meetings; visit the whites who were still available as well as the free blacks and mulattoes to get more information here and there and identify those among these groups of people apt to be recruited by the Indigenous Army. At that point, someone else approached them. As for the information coming from the opposing camp, there was always someone who, to make themselves seem interesting, under the influence of alcohol or wanting to impress young women, would let escape an important detail. Cécile had no qualms about seducing with her charms, as was described in one of the books that had come from England. Unlike Ferdinand, who had not really paid much attention to his English lessons, she could read English and even speak it, with an accent that she still didn't like. So, she had read *Pamela; or, Virtue Rewarded* in the original English, but she had been happy years later to find a French translation. She and Angeline had discussed it together, both wary of this love story that was too sentimental to be authentic between this young woman from a modest background and this man from the nobility, in whose home she was working. Outraged by the so-called Pamela, Angeline had said, "Shouldn't we think of her search for the improvement of her social status as opportunistic, as a type of prostitution?" While agreeing with her friend's opinion, Cécile had noted that some marriages in their milieu could also be considered legal prostitution. Like those of free blacks who had no money and married formerly enslaved women who'd received inheritances from their former masters, or impoverished mulattoes marrying free black women to refill their coffers. "It's like an agreement, the result of sometimes tense negotiations, not very romantic at all." This new expression, with its own baggage of passion, feelings, and emotions, appealed to them even when both parties knew that happy endings were by no means guaranteed. In fact, the romantic vision clashed with their mothers' good old common sense—mothers who had raised them with a practical view of married life to which they had to aspire. They saw all around them how some couples came into being. Meanwhile the two friends, feeling not quite ready, resisted the family pressure to find a husband, unlike many young women their age. But when night fell and she was alone, Cécile dreamed of a man with whom she'd feel good, without needing to hide her ideas, without wanting to please him at all costs. All around her, she only saw conventional people who were a little too much like her father, or they were carefree, and a little too much like her brother for her to take them seriously.

She'd name her firstborn daughter Sanite, because she had learned about the story of this captain who was executed along with her husband—this woman who wasn't afraid of death—she often thought about her. For weeks, all through the month of October, she was transported by Sanite's story, wanting to meet a witness to this scene. She had already heard stories about executions, but normally it was while spending time with groups of family or friends, during which ill-timed commentary would interrupt the retelling of the story, in which the exclamations of compassion or indignation would soften the blow of the horrors. At last, she met Gertrude, a woman who had been charged with resupplying the troops and who was also a healer. Gertrude didn't explain how she was able to witness the execution of Charles and Sanite Bélair, and Cécile knew from reading her face that it was impossible to ask her any questions about it. Sitting in a small, stuffy room, where the miserable rays of sun were meagerly playing with light on their faces, Cécile was gradually immersed in a world of gunpowder, the sounds of firearms, shouts, and shrieks. She followed the steps of the soldiers responsible for bringing the two prisoners in front of the firing squad. At some point she had wanted to tell this woman speaking in a monotonous voice to stop telling her story, but it seemed as though her lips had gotten stuck together. It was too late to stop the story. Silent and appalled, she followed the halting march of the men dragging Charles and Sanite. She heard the burst of machine-gun fire and the sound of the first body hitting the ground. Then, the determined voice, snapping like a slap in the face, refusing the blindfold: "I'm a soldier!" Insisting, still insisting with a hint of contempt, a touch of defiance. The silence that met the request, and the muffled sound of this second body, heavier than that of the rifles. Cécile relived this scene in her head, with misty eyes and a wildly beating heart, as she admired this woman who had not been afraid to face death, who didn't want preferential treatment based on the excuse that she could give birth.

Since then Cécile had become more determined to participate more actively in the struggle, especially since high society life in the city of Au Cap had become almost nonexistent. Theaters and parties continued, but with fewer people. Normally, Cécile and her brother would go especially to private balls hosted by acquaintances. The Lespinasse family hosted some as well, and their black, mulatto, and white friends were all invited. But the arrival of General Leclerc's expedition affected the relationships among the different groups, and the cultural and high society activities had slowed down greatly. Au Cap, considered to be the "Paris" of Saint-Domingue, had put away its sequins. Her mother often spoke to her about the time when balls, exhibits, and shows occurred on a regular basis. The population who could afford to go to dances, dressed in finery for balls that would begin at five in the afternoon and were supposed to end at nine in the evening but sometimes, even often, would last all night. Esther Lespinasse had also talked about the soirées in Vaux-Hall or the famous Coliseum of Master Pamelart. At the beginning, the Coliseum was not open to people of color, but since they could pay their entrance and were quite numerous, Pamelart, who was looking to get rich quickly, gave them permission to dance on Sundays only. Carnival was the liveliest period, with subscription balls being held in the city. And again, free blacks and mulattoes were not always allowed to attend. At the Comédie, they had to stay in their box seats to watch the whites dance. Cécile still felt the force of her mother's resentment when she talked about it years later.

And yet, the young woman would repeat to herself, that despite everything, they were the privileged ones. Despite the frustrations, their destiny seemed like a dream compared to those who had experienced capture and slavery. After all, the story of the ancestor Victorine ended up rather well—especially for those of her generation, whose childhood had taken place in a well-padded cocoon, well-protected from the daily reality of discrimination and injustice: private tutoring, good education, studies abroad. She was privileged, and in her mind her responsibility was greater because of it. Cécile was exploding with the need to act so that everyone would be free and equal, so that no one would be forced to work for the profit of others. She knew that men and women were fighting. Sanite Bélair was an extraordinary model, but there were others like her who fought, who died. With a special pride, Cécile was thinking again about the feats of the women whose stories circled back to her—the woman in the South who, with a firm hand, had placed around her own neck the rope that was to hang her. Another woman who, standing before the firing squad, tearfully told her daughters: "Rejoice, your hips will not give birth to slaves!" Or she thought about the women who had fought enemy troops while carrying mattresses to protect themselves from musket fire. So many acts of an almost unimaginable courage. How could Cécile still enjoy the privilege of being an educated woman when her uncle Emmanuel would call out those "armchair protesters"? He had been really irritated with her for calling him an enslaver and had used this expression during one of their discussions that pushed each of them to retreat to their respective corners. For once, she hadn't found a satisfactory response, and it was her mother who ended their verbal sparring. Nevertheless, Cécile never forgot those words, and since the Sanite Bélair incident, they resonated even more deeply with her.

Guillaume tried hard not to look at her, but each of her movements seemed to provoke an impulse within him, as he felt his whole being turn toward her. By his side, Désirée who seemed to have forgotten her sadness, was skipping and babbling, with small flowers in her hands that she had picked along the way. From time to time, while laughing she'd try to take off her friend's scarf to slip a flower in her hair, but her friend would hide it, gently. Finally, she put one behind the young woman's ear. This little yellow flower clashed with her casual but plain outfit: brown pants, a light blue tunic, a brown scarf, an armful of bracelets made of red and black pearls, frizzy black hair that escaped from the scarf, close to the nape of her neck. He felt the ill-timed desire to touch her with his fingers.

He jumped, because she had asked him a question, which he was quick to answer. She was no frills, and the questions were flying one after another: Why? Who? Where? What do you want to do with Boulet? She listened to the explanations, with her head slightly bent, and took a moment to react with a host of details about what they were planning to do. Guillaume was very surprised to see how much it pleased him to be included in this "we" that she used with authority. Désirée would follow her and the group's soldiers. The little one would be safe over there, and that oaf Boulet wouldn't find her. If he becomes a threat, we can get rid of him.

It was a sharp, clear voice. He felt it descend in him as if it knew where to settle. There, close to the wounds that had never healed, like the softness of Ma Aza's honey-soaked balms soothing his childhood scrapes. Between two painful memories that he thought he'd forgotten, her voice intervened—like a feathery but steady caress. It's as if she knew and was taking his hand in hers.

All week, he carried her within him. She agreed that he accompany them to a crossroads. Then she told him to turn around and leave. When he'd finally turned, they had disappeared in the woods. Surprisingly, he hadn't hesitated to let her leave with Désirée, first because he knew his sister, and the trust with which she followed the young woman clearly showed the strong and solid bond that connected them—even though he wondered where and how they'd met. And it was because he trusted her, too.

She had told him:

"Actually, what do you want me to call you? I'm Marie Nago."

"Me, I'm Guillaume Gillot."

"I'll find you, Guillaume the Griffe."

And for a whole week he had waited for a sign from her. Then she surfaced on the side of the road and started walking quietly alongside him. Désirée had stayed behind at the camp. It wasn't time for her to be seen yet.

The conversation went straight to the heart of things. With her, he understood that it would be different than it had been with the two women he'd courted. He knew he wouldn't get bored on this path that they were taking together, and that he wouldn't have to play the role of seducer. She smiled at one point, allowing him a glimpse into her interior world.

"Next week, maybe I'll bring you to the camp—unless you're too scared?"

"I'm not afraid."

I'm not crying. Tears are mixing with rain drops, changing their smell and taste. I'm completely soaked inside anyway; I have tears flowing beneath my skin. So they're not mixing with the rain drops that are falling on my face. I prefer the smell of rain. My tears taste like suffering and grief. I haven't cried since the day *Drooping Mouth* got to me, in Ma's absence.

Drooping Mouth is a coward and a good-for-nothing. That's the truth. Are you still afraid of him?

I was always afraid when he would get close to Ma Aza. The sounds he made on her body made me sick to my stomach. I wondered if she could breathe like when little Blaise stayed open-mouthed. Do you remember that? He made strange sounds and his eyes would roll. Edmond, the coachman, would hurry to slap him on the back, and little Blaise would finally cry out, expelling from deep within something pink and round. I would imagine Ma Aza lying beneath the planter Boulet, with her eyes turned upside down. He didn't stop shaking her, going up and down, grunting, but nothing escaped Ma Aza's mouth, and still she wouldn't speak. I would cry every time he climbed on top of her. I would sob and tremble so much that Ma would get up immediately to console me. So, Boulet got into the habit of taking her with him, and I would cry even more. Cry louder. And Ma refused to follow him because I was crying.

Désirée, you can't forget Drooping Mouth. And I can't forget my story. The two young boys dragged me outside, under the banana trees. I still remember them to this day. If I turn my head to the right, their faces mix in with the leaves; if I turn my head to the left, their faces get mixed in with the bunches of green fruit. I can close my eyes, but then I hear their voices, which scare me even more. So, I try to look at parts of the sky through the banana trees that surround us. They hurt me, they hurt me so much with their fingers, with their penises that I dig my nails in my flesh so as not to scream. I don't want to yell. That wouldn't help because no one will hear me where they are. No one will rescue me. Then, a long time afterward, they leave me alone, like a dying stem after the flower has blossomed. Me neither, just like you, I don't want to cry. Don't tell me, Désirée, that I have to lower my voice, that I'm frightening the two children. Yes, it's true that I always feel like hitting someone. It's better than hurting myself, like your mother used to do. You know very well that she would burn her skin, no doubt it was to erase *Drooping Mouth*'s smell. But that didn't work; instead, she should have burned that mean and stupid man who loved to play "the good guy" when other people were around. He never loved you; he was always jealous of the love she had for you. Ma Aza had lost the baby that was his and stopped getting pregnant after that—all that gnawed at him. He must have wondered if she had done it on purpose; he knew that she would have done anything for you. When he got close to you, his eyes would blaze with anger. He never touched you, but I know he would have done nothing to protect you either. Just like he did nothing on that day when those men dragged me under the banana trees.

I saw them leave, Fatima. But it was too late. I know they hurt you.

The planter Boulet knew it too, but he did nothing.

Boulet is rotten to the core. He attacks children. He caught me by the arm when Ma wasn't there. He pressed his mouth close to my face and whispered in my ear: "If you cry one more time when I'm with Aza, I'm going to sell you and you'll never see your mother again. So, shut up, don't cry, and don't say anything to anyone." I was so afraid that day that I noticed that my hands were trembling. Since then, I no longer cry. I didn't cry when I found you under the banana trees. I can no longer cry. He didn't hit me, he didn't hurt me like those young men who attacked you, but I got so scared. I can no longer cry.

Anyway, my little Désirée, believe me, crying is useless.

I didn't know that my body could climb the Puilboreau mountain backward without getting tired, flying all the way to Plaisance, cross Bas-Limbé without going through Port Margo. I never knew that the beauty of the world could be held in my hands, shine on my skin, and reach my eyes. All the noise burst in me, the feverish tickling of grass, the buzzing of insects, a puff of wind on my sex. I didn't know that dying so slowly could be so gentle, that life could fade in a gulf of pleasure.

I, who never trembled with fear, I suddenly doubted the sturdiness of my legs. They gave way when confronted with the magnitude of my desire. I had to breathe the same air as Guillaume, I had to touch the ground where he placed his feet so that I could feel myself becoming Marie Nago ten times stronger, a hundred times stronger, a hundred times more beautiful, a hundred times more alive.

When I got closer to him that day, the first thing that came to mind was that he no longer had bowed legs; then our eyes met, and I knew that my life had just changed. I didn't yet know how, but already I knew that the wind that made my skin shiver was not coming from the trees.

We saw each other every day and that was barely enough. I would have wanted to be this small leaf brushing against his neck, or this trivial insect that he'd casually swat away with a hand, this new tune that he would hum, that escaped his lips without knowing it existed only because of him.

The men from the group smirked when they saw us together, not out of unkindness, but because one had to find some enjoyment when death was everywhere. Life and death were constantly in tandem, and we were in their midst. To dance with life and death, to wait and see which was the strongest, which would keep us close: the sun or the eternity of silence. Our laughter exploded like an armor of light. It created a ring of sparks, our steps sounding like grenades.

The first time I brought him to the camp, a woman passed a stray hand on Guillaume's backside, and several people burst into laughter. I felt his hand shiver in mine, then he looked at my friends' naughty faces and smiled. In a confident gesture, he embraced me and held me tight. Ah! We understand. You're keeping your little griffe, Marie Nago.

None of my relationships had prepared me for this tidal wave in which I eagerly submerged myself, as if I had been waiting for it my entire life. I fed myself with tenderness, giving it, receiving it, in the palm of my hands in the rainy season, in my eyelashes in the dry sunny season. I wasn't even surprised at this abrupt and radical transformation. Casting off my well-known characteristic detachment, I now felt a sudden clarity that gave my gestures an almost tender flair. I had already accepted my affection for Désirée as an anomaly connected to the little one's unpredictable behavior. A "little one" who was merely two years younger than I was, but I felt so old when I watched her smile. When I told Guillaume that I was older than him, he said that age had nothing to do with the number of years one has lived. In his view, he and I were the same age even if, according to their ledgers, I was born four years before him. Could he be right after all? I would often wonder if Désirée wouldn't always remain a child, with her sad eyes searching for tenderness, incapable of understanding why life sometimes hurt so much.

The group had accepted her immediately. Several recognized her, having seen her before in the mountains, camouflaged in the branches of a tree, or simply lying down to soak her feet in the river. The few who were distrustful of her at first decided later that she was harmless even though they continued to complain about her presence. Scarves of all colors, skipping legs, unexpected bursts of laughter, curious whisperings, became a part of camp life. Désirée even took a few self-defense lessons with Master Silo, before turning them into dance classes in which she led the big man in a series of complicated steps that he soon performed with grace and speed. "She makes us smile, your little one," he told me one day. "But I see so much sadness in her eyes that I could behead those who hurt her."

Sometimes, the little one disappeared only to return a few days later. I never questioned her. That wouldn't have worked with Désirée. But my heart was always in torment when she left because I knew that she was going away to seek refuge from pain. She was alone, like an animal in agony. What pain was she hiding?

I shared the murderous rage of Master Silo in thinking of those who had hurt Désirée. And most of all, when sparring with him I never forgot that he could chop off limbs with a machete. In fact, he had cut off a great number of them during skirmishes with the French. With my own eyes, I had watched him cut off a shoulder without hesitating, and the disciple in me had admired and envied the dexterity of his movements—their speed and precision, the fall of the leg, the sudden advance of the torso. Would I be able to be as fast and skillful one day? For now, I was training as much as possible. I wasn't yet able to handle the machete as well as I did the baton, but I was learning how to use the bayonet. There was no way I'd be beaten without fighting to the very end. I was even more attached to life now that happiness had nestled in me, now that the sight of a single human being could change the color of the sky, that a single voice spoke a thousand languages within me, each one bringing a new alphabet, more mysterious than the books I had learned to decode, more passionate than the words the old people used to make us practice.

Mysterious words that I repeated mechanically. My friend Bayi was a believer, and I envied sometimes this trancelike state she'd enter during ceremonies.

One night, I attended an initiation ceremony that old Lola had organized. The negroes were singing and clapping as they surrounded two women and a man who were dressed in white, which indicated their commitment.

Sojème
Eh eh Bomba hen hen
Canga bafio té
Canga moun délé
Canga do ki la
Canga li

Master Silo was at the ceremony and seemed transformed. His body swayed as he chanted, turning his baton, circulating among the initiated, taking a gulp of rum from time to time, then starting to sing again. He'd look at me sometimes, but I wondered if he saw me. I had never seen him in such a state.

Conga do ki la
Canga li

I, too, had begun to dance, without realizing it. The music was flowing in me, leading me and I let myself go, without holding back. It felt good to feel my body so alive, so hot. Sweat seeped between my breasts, traveling down the length of my ribs, continuing onto my belly, and I felt it slide down to my underpants, go along my thighs like mischievous fingers, and I'd jump, with my skirt sticking to my legs, my blouse clinging to my chest, trampling on war, fear, suffering, and death.

Conga do ki la
Canga li

With Guillaume, pleasure is better, softer, hotter, more titillating than sweat. He's everywhere, he embraces me, he twirls me around, he throws me in the air, he catches me, he lays me on a silk cloth, places me against the bark of a tree. I see the fire at the big ceremony, the first rays of sunshine on the hilltop, and I feel the rain washing me with big sprays of water. I feel free from all pain, and I suffer. I laugh and I cry. I am alive.

Jérôme had hardly slept since some friends told him about the Battle of Crête-à-Pierrot. The sad cruelty of his own fate haunted him. Caught up in the vast wave of bravery that was spreading all around him, among the opinionated whites who encouraged his father to stay and fight to protect his property, among the mulattoes who insisted on defending their interests and privileges, among the free blacks who felt threatened, and among the great number of formerly enslaved blacks who did not want to become slaves again. This French expedition that had landed had spread a wave of violent reactions in everyone. There were the whites who thought the expedition would restore order, get rid of bandits, put Saint-Domingue back in the hands of the French. And others for whom this expedition was like an exterminating army coming to destroy the blacks, guilty or not guilty of rebellion, and would work twice as hard to sweep away the people of color who complicated the situation by their very existence.

Amid this flurry of demands and fierce declarations of bravery, Jérôme felt like a fraud who'd be exposed at any moment. Would his father be the first to come and expose the fear and detachment of his offspring? Would it be his mother, who had brought from her land of origin a head held high, who seemed from the outset to condemn his lack of boldness? For once, he was happy to be so far away from his brother and sister, who were in France and couldn't confuse him. Julien knew him as well as Sophie did, and both would have noticed his indecisiveness. But his so-called friends, mulattoes like himself, were for the most part too absorbed by their pompous declarations to see how he kept himself apart, how his appreciation was unclear, how words would only cross his lips too late as apprehension filled the silence between him and them. There must be other men who, like him, hid their fears and their mixed feelings about being killed in battle, right? Weren't there men who would have wanted to live, like him, just ignorant and quiet, without having to fight to express their ideas, without expecting the world to follow their indulgences?

He admired the bravery of those who risked their lives in battle. Along with others in the group, he had listened to the story of the Battle of Crête-à-Pierrot. The fearless men and women who ran in front of the shell fire, those who stepped over the lifeless bodies of their companions to keep fighting against the twelve thousand Frenchmen sent by the expeditionary army to recapture the fort. Though the Indigenous Army had to evacuate in the end, it resisted successive attacks from the French army with remarkable courage. Jérôme couldn't help but be proud, not only of Lamartinière and this Marie-Jeanne about whom so many witnesses were talking, but of all the people who had fought. But he also told himself that it was insane to fight against this expeditionary army that had so many armed men who were better equipped and determined to reinstate slavery. Even if a good number among them had already succumbed to the heat, to yellow fever, to their diminishing food reserves; even if their shoes were fraying and some of them, according to his friends, had to beg for food—would that be enough to convince them to leave, to abandon the fight? Also, Rochambeau, who had replaced Leclerc, seemed fierce and uncompromising. Undoubtedly, they were following the orders received from Bonaparte to control the rebellion at all costs and reestablish colonial order in Saint-Domingue! And finally, what did they care about the number of victims, whether innocent or guilty, mulattoes or blacks!

Zinga sighed with relief when he found her dancing in the middle of Moussa's group. Even if he was probably skeptical of these groups who had supported the generals-in-chief, if only for a short time, he knew that Désirée was safe with them. In fact, since the expedition's arrival and even before, most of the blacks understood that the whole group of cultivators and generals-in-chief, black or of color, didn't always share the same goals. One saw them everywhere, these generals, whether it was Christophe, or Toussaint before the French tied him up like a baby goat, or Dessalines—but for Zinga, the real leaders were leaders like him, those who worked in the shadows—even though not all the rebels were always in agreement. Years of captivity had created discord that was sometimes baseless. Those who had worked on the sugar plantations didn't get along with those from the coffee plantations; the field workers distrusted house slaves; Creoles and Africans were pitted against each other; those who spoke a few words of French felt superior to those who only spoke languages from before the crossing. Yet despite all this, Zinga thought that the future of Saint-Domingue rested on these groups. They were supported by most of the people: the ones who worked in the fields, who had bent under the yoke of the French, and who now wanted neither slavery, nor compromise, nor negotiation.

Negotiation was a word Zinga hated. Could freedom be negotiated? Near Dondon, he had met an old black man who had negotiated his freedom with his former masters. He was so enfeebled that his bones cracked like dried twigs, his hands barely able to hold onto the walking stick he leaned on. What use was his negotiated freedom when he'd worked for years like a condemned animal in the sugarcane fields—when leaving his hut in the morning made his entire body tremble, when the first evening mist, deadly cold, slipped into his old bones? What use was it when his glassy eyes could barely see the sunrise and the whiff of crushed sugarcane obscured all the new smells that surrounded him? Every hour, every day spent enslaved had marked a portion of his skin, which he could no longer get rid of. After all these years, the marks had taken over, and his freedom so dearly negotiated didn't know where to take root.

Zinga hid further behind the trees to better observe Désirée. He was surprised to never tire of seeing her. How he'd changed! Was it because of this young woman who looked like a wounded little bird that he'd gotten attached to this island? Was it because of her that the sea didn't just look like a shifting space in which he could get lost, but instead it looked like a myriad of enchanting colors? Was it because of her that the mountains seemed to whisper stories about the gliding wind and the simmering fog? Was it only because of her that he wanted to fight so that this land would belong to those whose sweat, tears, and blood had been shed to nourish and enrich it? For so long, he had focused only on his own fate, observing with detachment, if not with cynicism, the conflicts around him, watching with curiosity the Africans or the Creoles who threw themselves in the struggle with a determination and conviction that he felt eluded him. Yet here he was now, next to them, leading a group of determined combatants to go all the way. It's as if meeting Désirée had clarified the needs he'd buried since his arrival on the island.

Leaving his leaf-covered refuge, Zinga had barely moved when he saw Marie Nago come closer to Désirée, in quick and sure steps. The young griffe from the Martineau plantation, who had, according to reports, earned the grade of second lieutenant in the Indigenous Army, had also intervened, a silent and adamant warning in his movements. In fact, without realizing it, undoubtedly because looking for her and then seeing her had relaxed his self-protective and defensive instincts, Zinga was surrounded by them all. He thought he'd found the camp, but he'd made it to its very center, as in an ambush. A lean, muscular man was observing him from afar, but Zinga recognized the old warrior's attack posture, and he'd caught sight of the baton he was gripping in his right hand. Another woman had appeared to his left and, with a mocking laugh, was spinning her machete nonchalantly.

"I've come for Désirée," he said simply, his arms visibly open, though instinctively Marie Nago and Guillaume came closer to the young woman. Putting down the puppy she was playing with, she then turned toward him, her half-lit eyes filled with an even heavier sadness. He felt a disconcerting urgency to absorb all the misfortune that was whirling in her by holding her close. But she was already bursting into a happy laugh and huddling in his arms like a happy child. "Zinga, you came. I told you he would come." And then three of them looked at each other, knowing that she wasn't talking to any of them.

Cécile considered these last few months to be the longest period of her life, and she wondered what the rest of 1803 had in store for them. Already the month of April had begun with the news of Toussaint's death at Fort de Joux. Would it be another year full of conflicts, of new twists and turns, with days that would bring their share of anguish, months that would see still more terror without any resolution to the conflicts? Would there be an end this year? What would it be?

In order not to succumb to this permanently tense atmosphere that hung over the house, the city, and the island, the young woman continued to record the events and her feelings in her journal. Trying to bring order to this uncontrollable present. A present so weighty that it made it impossible to learn anything from turning to the past. A present so turbulent that the future became an illusion that was impossible to contemplate.

Sometimes she'd return to earlier journal entries, leafing through pages covered in her refined girlish handwriting, having learned to shape cursive letters, to respect the rules of French grammar to clearly express her thoughts. The first pages of 1802 brought her back to the New Year's festivities, celebrated this time at her uncle Emmanuel's house. The entire family had gathered there on Christmas Eve for a weeklong stay on the plantation in Haut-Limbé, trying to maintain a semblance of normality in a situation that was becoming more and more incendiary. Uncle Pierre had stopped by briefly, then returned home the same day. Ferdinand had returned to Au Cap before the end of the year to spend New Year with his girlfriend Emma. Fortunately, his parents didn't make a big deal of it. At any rate, to avoid the typical disputes between Cécile and her uncle Emmanuel, her mother had insisted that the discussions be focused on fashion—given that Cécile's father had been able to get some recent catalogs from Paris—and on the newborn in the family. Emmanuel's oldest son, Matthieu Lespinasse, and his wife, Georgette, had just had a baby, a son named Claude-Pierre Lespinasse—the firstborn of his generation, and everyone was gushing over the little boy. Holding him against her, taking in the smell of talcum powder, Cécile had wondered if she'd ever experience this joy. Even while whispering sweet words to the baby, she knew that this wasn't a priority for her, not yet. Not like her friend Marcelle, who was willing to do anything to get pregnant, even if it meant marrying the first one to come along and get her pregnant.

According to her journal, it was in February that she'd learned about the arrival of the expedition that took place at the end of January. Since then, bad news had followed at an alarming rate. First, the death of the two brothers of her friend Angeline when Rochambeau seized Fort Dauphin. Angeline never recovered from that. Then, of course, there was Crête-à-Pierrot. Dessalines and Christophe had surrendered to the French while keeping their military ranks. Many people of color and blacks had been massacred.

Her brother, whom she thought of as a cynical libertine, would mock her indignation at the way the French treated Louverture. Even if Cécile didn't approve of all of Louverture's tactics, she couldn't accept that the French had humiliated him to the extent that they did. For his part, Ferdinand found the general both naive and arrogant. How could he have trusted those who thought that blacks were inferior to whites and who wanted to reinstate slavery?

The days brought with them so many events that she couldn't always keep track, despite her decision to methodically make note of the most important ones.

Without wanting to, she stopped at the page in her journal that seemed to be waiting for her glance. It was the day she'd met Amédée. She had finally felt a wriggling sensation, a swarming of the senses, an irrepressible desire for a body pressed against her own. She'd been waiting for this moment for so long: to finally experience this feeling that her married friends would talk about knowingly, sometimes with pride and joyfulness, sometimes with sadness and mystery. Angeline, when she was still laughing, would say that the tone used reflected the kind of lover the husband was. Now Cécile could no longer confide in her best friend. The young woman had decided to join the front lines too. Anger and rage had overtaken her. Nothing could hold her back: not her family's pleas, not the wet kisses of her sister's first baby, to whom she was godmother.

That day, Cécile had visited her friend at the camp. Not to try to convince her to come home, but to see if her pain has lessened a bit, and if her friendship could help calm her. Despite her worry, she understood Angeline's need to act in the name of her two brothers, whom she'd loved dearly. Besides, the encampment's ambience hardly lent itself to long and intimate conversations. Fascinated, Cécile took in the turbulent atmosphere that reigned under the shed where the military had assembled. Comments, orders, the noise of weapons that were being put away, the mess tins that were banging together, the smell of powder and sweat, the eyes heavy from built-up fatigue, the hardened lips, the uniforms, the hats, the ammunition—she was drawn to everything. She was intoxicated with the fever that was spreading all around her, filling the space with an energy that she swallowed in big gulps.

When Angeline indifferently introduced her to Amédée, Cécile had barely raised her eyes in his direction. Angeline pulled her by the arm. "Cécile, listen to me!" In a calm and determined tone, her friend had given her final instructions. "You'll explain to my parents . . . I'm entrusting you with my godson . . . Everything is written on this sheet. I know I can count on you. It's possible that I won't come back alive. There are many losses on this side, and on theirs as well." Cécile opened her mouth, but Angeline had already turned her back. She saw her silhouette blend in with the others in uniform.

She suddenly realized that someone was looking at her. His name came to her: Amédée, a leader of the African group. Through her tears, she watched him. Between them, at that moment, she felt a light and indescribable current, an unavoidable and instantaneous attraction. Though indecisive and overwhelmed by her best friend's departure, she couldn't look away, and stood there fixed, waiting for what was to come next.

I don't like you telling me what to do, Fatima. Your mouth is full of harsh words that hurt when I say them. Ma Aza would say that those who enjoy hurting others are often in a great deal of pain without knowing it.

I know very well that I'm in pain, Désirée, but you're rambling with your advice, your proverbs, your sayings, and your false smiles. Your springy steps and your somersaults will lead you nowhere.

Gilles, stop crying, my little one. Don't listen to Fatima. Your mother will come pick you up later, I promise. One day, I heard her tell Ma Aza that only her love for you kept her alive, that for you she'd be willing to accept anything, to walk barefoot on hot coals, to cross a river without knowing how to swim, to make the trip from Africa to Saint-Domingue, if necessary, to be with you. Death can't stand up to love.

Désirée, you've been speaking only about love since meeting this Zinga, this big-footed African. Sometimes you ignore us, Gilles and me. I overheard the African speak to you about his country of mists and lakes, telling you that his mother had doe-like eyes and that his brothers must be grown men by now. I saw him touch you, kiss you cautiously as if you were made of porcelain, like the plates that were in the locked oak cupboard. It always made me sad to see the little pink flowers against a white background in the cupboard's darkness. What a waste! If we own beautiful objects, we should see them and enjoy them. At night with Caleb, we'd sit and look at the sky, and he would say that counting the stars is like touching specks of happiness. Caleb would tell me that together we would reach the top of the mountain to better see the stars. We never did it.

The big-footed African, that was a good name you gave him, Virginie. But you and Gilles should stop your shenanigans. Between Désirée who's in love and the little Gilles who's whining nonstop, and you, Virginie, who mention your brother's name every second and a half, my ears and eyes, nose and hands—my entire body ends up exhausted when I see you, when I hear you, when I feel your presence around me and within me. I want you to get out of here, and fast. Go away!

I have a right to talk about Caleb. He was my brother, my protector, my friend. When Ma died, I only had him, he only had me. He'd tell me that he wouldn't always be at Boulet the planter's and that we'd go settle in the hills, him and me. I don't know where he is, but I'll will find him one day.

Me too, I'll find my mother. I'm crying because I think of her all the time, and I'm waiting for her to return. She promised me she'd never leave. I don't know why she lied.

And there they go again, the two of them complaining. I want my Ma, I want Caleb. Listen children, life is hard. We must get used to it.

You're starting to get on my nerves, Fatima. You're hurting the children. You're not the only one to have suffered. We each have our portion of misfortune. What's different with you is that you want the entire world to carry the weight of yours.

Guillaume had already experienced physical pain. When he was seven, he had fallen more than three feet from a tree and hurt his arm. The pain was terrible, and the plantation's doctor was not tender in treating him. A fever epidemic in the workhouses had kept him sufficiently busy. Deriding his tears, his grandfather had at first left him with the cook, then exasperatedly asked the planter Martineau's permission to call for Bashira. Having been exempted from the workhouse to care for the little griffe whom no one wanted, Bashira had cradled him, given him a potion to drink, wrapped him in leaves from the almond tree, and he'd fallen asleep against her chest, inhaling the smell of molasses that seemed to imbue the woman in those times. When he woke up, Désirée was beside him, asleep with her mouth partially opened, a frail arm around him like a soft and gentle veil.

Now he realized that this almost twenty-year-old pain couldn't be compared to the ripping sensation that was burning his abdomen. Seeing his own blood flow seemed strange to him, as if he had split in two and was watching another man's blood stain the ground a brownish red that would soon be mixing with the grass. Then he thought of that distant day when Désirée had made their blood gush out on the thin gravel, and smiled despite himself. At least, he thought he'd smiled, then heard Marie Nago, detected the trembling in her voice, but also felt the force of her hands lifting his head and placing it softly on her lap. The relief he felt made his eyelids close.

When he opened them again, Marie Nago was still by his side, crouched on the ground, seemingly asleep but smiling at him with closed eyes: "So, Guillaume le Griffe." She'd gotten used to calling him that, and he really like it, this name that dignified and played upon the nickname he'd had since childhood. "So, are you finally waking up?" She took his hand, and they stayed a long moment saying sweet nothings—things both useless and important that sometimes surface in moments of great emotion.

This is how Désirée found them. Entering the tent quickly, wearing a red scarf around her hair, she seemed to have forgotten to wear the radiant smile that didn't always conceal her helplessness. Seeing her younger brother, her eyes brightened, a sliver of infinite tenderness, opening them to the light. She murmured and shook her head from side to side. Marie Nago tried in vain to keep her next to them. She left as quickly as she'd entered.

"Leave her alone," murmured Guillaume. "My sister is hurting, and I can't do anything about it. You know, Ma Aza always said that Désirée had physically withstood all the evils that kill children here: lockjaw, diphtheria, yellow fever. From the time she'd been on that ship of misfortune, she'd clung to the maternal womb so as not to disappear. But all these victories over illnesses had cost her, because now she has no more strength to fight off others: the internal ones, which are the most dangerous. Her physical resistance has consumed all her strength. Mentally, she's become fragile. Other people's distresses fall on her shoulders and swallow her whole."

While still a child, Guillaume had become aware of the sadness that often filled his sister's eyes. A surly and hard voice, blows from a riding crop on a horse's back, or the sobs from a child who'd been beaten, and Désirée's gaze would show her dread, fear, and suffering. The grief hidden under her skipping feet, her fanciful look, and her dazzling smile would grow larger as she heard about others' misfortunes. Guillaume remembered the day when he really understood that his sister lived in a different reality. That day, Ma Aza had cried out terribly, which had impelled Clara the cook to rush out of the house although she was so big that she almost never left her kitchen. With a pan in each hand, Clara had rushed as if she were holding two grenades, only to stop suddenly with the other people who had run up like her. In one second, they watched as Désirée dragged Fatima's lifeless body. A young woman's body, slender and supple, one that Guillaume had just seen the day before, playing with the younger children. Their eyes followed Fatima as they would follow the arc of a rainbow. How beautiful she was, Fatima! A long torso and a neck that moved with a still youthful elegance, slender legs that leapt often but rhythmically, embodying a nascent sensuality. Years afterward, Guillaume realized that he'd fallen in love with her, undoubtedly like all the other young people whose paths she'd crossed. She had a way of turning her head and smiling with a teasing look that urged people to follow her. How beautiful she was! She'd wear her blue flounce hem dress, with a white belt tied around the waist. Guillaume recognized the dress, but on that day, her hem was stained with blood. Désirée, who was smaller than the young woman, was dragging the lifeless body as she staggered, puffed, and panted. She refused to let go of her. The manager had to forcibly take Fatima away from her. And at that point, Désirée let herself fall to the ground without saying a word, without shedding a tear.

Fatima died of excessive bleeding caused by the multiple rapes she had endured. The doctor had mentioned vaginal and anal tears, as well as lacerations. Désirée had apparently found her. Did she witness the crime? Did she see these men commit their abominable acts in front of the eyes of a young girl? Ma Aza had always thought she had been witness to something. For a whole month, the girl child had had terrible nightmares and would scream in her sleep. But she never wanted to say anything to her mother. And when Guillaume dared to ask, she would pirouette and say, "Oh, little brother, why do you want to talk about that now?"

A few weeks after Fatima's death, the two sons of planter Boulet's neighbor were pelted with stones during a hunting game. A projectile hit one of them on the ear and the other had his lip split open. Guillaume suspected that Désirée had something to do with this, but he was so afraid of attracting attention to her that he didn't say a word to anyone and didn't ask her any more questions.

Huddled up against Guillaume, Marie Nago would listen to him talk about Désirée, about their childhood, about the two women who had fed them and protected them. From time to time, the young man would doze off, carried away by the potions that she made him drink. When he woke up, he'd search immediately with his eyes and hands, to reassure himself that she was there. This was because he knew that the one who in so short a time had taken so large a place in his universe was also facing death in the form of a cocked bayonet, the angry traits of a soldier determined to kill at all costs, or the precise movements of a man hidden behind a tree. He knew that Marie Nago could have been in his place, that she too could have gotten a bullet in the abdomen, that she could have died. The thought made him shudder, and he pushed the intolerable image away from his mind.

Gritting his teeth against the pain that would surge from time to time, breaking through the potion's impermanent protection, he preferred to remember his encounter with his own mortality. With his still-parched lips, he told Marie Nago about their march, which had started strong and assured but became more and more halting in the gullies and on the hills, first under a crushing sun, then a driving rain.

"We had to find Captain Moreau's brigade, which needed reinforcement. As second lieutenant, I led the troops, feeling proud but so burdened with responsibility. But I walked, encouraging the others, keeping to myself the fear of the potential risks run by these men who were my responsibility. We had to bypass the Fort-Liberté station that the French had recaptured at the beginning of the year. There was another path, but it was much longer. Then, the scout warned us of suspicious sounds a few kilometers ahead of the fort. A French brigade made up of whites, mulattoes, and some blacks attempted to surround us. The battle was ferocious. They were armed with sabers, bayonets, and rifles. We had rifles and machetes. One of their men, a young mulatto who was barely twenty years old, hurled himself toward us with his saber, striking my companion on my right with a terrible force. I saw him sway and then slump against a tree. His head was hanging strangely. Then suddenly, a rifle shot hit the mulatto, who also fell. I was facing and surrounded by cadavers and I, too, struck like a madman. I felt neither fatigue nor fear—focusing only on marking my target, striking a blow, avoiding sabers, dodging bayonets. When it was over, the grass was stained with blood, corpses were lying on top of each other in an almost indecent heap. I had lost thirteen men out of the sixty who were under my command. The French troops beat a retreat and we were able to proceed with our course to find Captain Moreau's brigade. It's only upon arriving that I realized I was bleeding, and the pain knocked me out."

"And as soon as you were in a state to be transported, they brought you here," Marie Nago concluded, not wanting to relive the panic that overtook her when she saw the men returning, two days earlier than expected, with a pale and crushed Guillaume. Even when someone confirmed that no vital organ had been affected, simply seeing him hurt had thrown her into an anguish that had darkened the world.

Apparently asleep, Guillaume was imagining the faces of those who had fallen on both sides, blood shedding, life fleeing as if it had not just been present seconds before, leaving nothing behind—except for open and empty eyes, gaping mouths without breath. The question that worried him, that prevented him from resting: "How many more lives were going to cease before the end?"

I was so surprised to remember my mother's smile that I became short of breath for a moment—or at least that's what Guillaume said afterward. With this smile, the smell of her arms returned—a smell of grilled peanuts that filled my memory with other moments: the taste of well-salted yam on my tongue, the scent of onions, the lingering smell of peppers on my skin when my father would kiss me.

I had seen the tenderness that was in Guillaume's eyes when he spoke about Ma Aza and Ma Bashira. He kept mentioning their names, as if he wanted me to know them too, so that they weren't completely gone from his life. I became fond of these women whom I didn't know when they were alive. In his smile, I saw the tenderness swell when he spoke of them. His love seemed to travel from Aza to Bashira or to Désirée, neither diminishing nor dwindling. Gradually, in the face of such spontaneous tenderness, I began to feel somewhat unmoored without knowing why. I was overcome with sadness, and I felt far away, suddenly different. But not completely. It was as if a part of me recognized this feeling of belonging, this feeling of a bond so strong that it would follow you everywhere, even when you think you've left it behind. I should have known that a great upheaval was brewing in me.

On that day, I was listening to Guillaume tell me for the umpteenth time, but with so much spirit and affection, how Ma Aza invented a story for each child under her care. He'd tell me how her generally flat voice would change to imitate animals, plants, and humans, creating an enchanting world where the young girl no longer saw the curved back and the hands of her mother, where the young boy would forget his father's fatigue and irritation. Ma Aza became the river, the moon, the vines that carried the children elsewhere, enveloping them in magic and tenderness. Sometimes, she'd talk about animals they didn't know, describe mysterious landscapes that made her own eyes radiant; so they opened wide their own eyes and accepted the unknown with a captivated eagerness, without an adult's petty suspicion.

Is that why, without any other hint except for a pang of the heart, suddenly I also became a child obsessed with Aza's story? I saw myself as a small child, before the ship, before the crossing, before the shipping ledger, before receiving the name Marie Nago. I found myself running toward my mother and I heard her laughter. And this laughter went straight to my heart, where it made an immense hole, through which I went down in free fall. I can't settle anywhere. Pain awaits me without any compromise, without a parachute to save me. She'd been waiting for me for so long. A cry escapes my lips, a powerful cry that breaks me in half, and I find myself upside down, with my head bowed, cut into pieces each as bloody as the other. This laughter brings me back to the time before their shipping ledgers, and I can no longer look directly at the sky. I'm in too much pain. Guillaume's arms embrace me—so hard that air can barely get back in, which is all the better, given that in the span of a second I no longer want this air. I push him away and enclose myself in this elsewhere that brings me close to myself.

"Marie, my love, please."

"Akissi, my name is Akissi."

"I don't care. Marie Nago, you're the one I love, not your name."

She got on the ship with me, but she never made it to Saint-Domingue. The waves were turbulent, we were tossed around like parcels. One woman's leg would shift two steps away from my neck, hitting me from time to time. So my shoulder collided with the body of another unknown person. Ma was vomiting nonstop. She was all pale and trembling, I was holding on to her back. Every day, she became skinnier, disappearing before my very eyes. With every jolt of the ship, I felt her body shrink, becoming even more puny and vulnerable. Her shoulders seemed so skinny under the fabric that covered them that I avoided looking at them. She was coughing constantly, her back spasming. Her pain went through my own body, and I pressed myself softly against her, since I didn't want to hurt her by squeezing too hard. Then, one day I woke up and no longer felt her body against mine.

When the ship drew alongside the port of Cap, I was led to the market. A planter from Haut-Limbé put me in his batch. And in their ledger, I became Marie Nago.

His stint in the French Army taught Jérôme that time was defined only by the actions that one took. And those often depended on encounters, on individuals one met—through a simple gesture at times, a complicit or accusing look, or an ill-timed grimace. And then time stopped, and it seemed to last so long that looking at one's watch or at the sun was useless. Time passed with the rhythm of emotions, like lips that trembled to tell the experience of pain—one that's more powerful than the sound of the wind, the start of a pulse before announcing the end of life.

In the army, he fell into an unfamiliar world of emotions. The fear of not being up to par had always consumed him, but he discovered the terror not only of dying at any given moment but of dying like a dog on the battlefield, an anonymous corpse that one walks over to escape or a corpse against which one plays dead to fool the enemy. He experienced a growing indignation at not being able to control his fear, while some seemed to mock him for it. Each day became an endless nightmare from which he couldn't escape.

Yet in the beginning, he had felt relieved. With an appeasing personality, he followed orders and tried not to complain openly. He managed even to avoid the drudgery and the tasks that were too thankless. However, after two weeks, he was appointed to a new unit, and that's when doubt took over and his worry deepened.

His mother met the news of his decision without saying a word. He couldn't answer the question that he could read in her eyes. How could he admit to her that fear had dictated his choice, that his need for security had impelled him to join this army without much sense of belonging, without any conviction. He didn't answer but she'd undoubtedly seen the truth in his eyes. With a shrug of the shoulders, she cast it away, in the shadows, unambiguously without shame. As a pragmatic person, his father had then gone to see military friends for advice and recommendations. Before the end of the week, he had brought him to a sergeant, and then to a captain, who had filled both of their heads with everything he shouldn't do if he wanted to stay alive, and what he should do if he didn't want to annoy his superiors. No one had told him that the blacks in the unit would treat him with such disdain, as if he were an enemy among them, a traitor who should be hit often and randomly, an idiot who was mercilessly mocked, a captive whose execution was anticipated with jubilation. They were fifteen in all: eight blacks, two mulattoes, including himself and a certain Paul Duval, and five whites, including their commanding officer. He had soon understood that the whites distrusted the blacks, expecting any day they'd rebel against them. The officer in charge had gotten into the habit of starting to leave everything related to discipline to the two mulattoes, transforming them into middlemen subject to the soldiers' resentment and anger. Paul seemed to put up with it until the day when he disappeared, abandoning the troop. The blacks sniggered and Jérôme wondered why they were there, whether they were spying or waiting for an opportune moment to eliminate the whites. Oddly, he managed to withstand the physical inconveniences, the lack of food, the heat, the exhaustion, the painful feet, the days of not being able to wash up, and the uncomfortable proximity; but the mental solitude in which he found himself ate away at him. Always unable to make decisions, he spent another week like this on the alert and in an increasingly confusing state of mind.

    His courage surfaced when he no longer expected it. They had received orders to reach Saint-Marc. His unit had the unpleasant mission of fetching the condemned, who were supposed to be hanged. There were twenty-one of them. Already, with just the thought of rubbing shoulders with men who were going to be executed, Jérôme felt bile rise to his mouth. His stomach turned and he dared not look at his black companions because there were twenty-one negroes condemned for treason against France, for crimes and acts of barbarity against planters, for setting fires and other less reprehensible actions. Jérôme was part of the detachment that had to accompany the captain to the prison to get the negroes. That's when he learned that they couldn't be hanged, because there was only one gallows and one executioner. He was going to have to make many trips from the gallows, situated to the east of the city, all the way to the prison to bring back the condemned in groups of four. Before taking each one away from the gallows, the executioner's assistant waited for the strangulation to be completed. Jérôme would look at the shivering bodies, as the last breath of life beat against eternal immobility. He thought he'd vomit, piss on himself or even worse in front of the other soldiers, and make himself look even more ridiculous and pitiful, and that's when his eyes met those of one of the condemned. The man held himself straight, calm, and silent. The three others who had just come from prison were also quiet and determined, ready to die, as if losing their lives in this way was the most natural of circumstances. One beautiful February morning under a sky speckled with playful clouds, while the surrounding city carried on, despite the few activities that were still taking place there. A woman with a basket of fruit on her head was headed toward the market, which was less and less lively, and a man was washing his face in the fountain. Jérôme glanced in the distance from time to time, then brought his gaze back to the condemned men, swinging back and forth between two parallel universes, separated by several yards. He noticed once again the one whose gaze he'd met. Apparently lost in thought, he was looking straight ahead. Until the last moment, he remained stonily indifferent, impassible, refusing, like his comrades, the blindfold offered him. Such serenity emanated from him that Jérôme forgot his own fear and felt a charge of admiration and respect take its place, filling him with pride and courage. He didn't know that one could feel at once so empowered and so sad.

Jérôme reconsidered all the information that he had also heard and had himself peddled at a time that seemed suddenly far away: information on the group of rebels and on the African chiefs known as "bloody savages," thirsty for blood and vengeance. These twenty-one men who were all hanged in groups of four had not been tried. Kidnapped and tied up, they were put in prison to be assassinated without any due process. Who were the real savages? How to escape this cycle of violence? Wasn't it too late to prevent the bloodshed?

In this war, France counted on the people of color. Because they'd received equal rights from the French Legislative Assembly in April 1792, France seemed to expect their loyal service. But hadn't they fought for these rights? After all, Ogé and Chavannes had paid with their lives, since their execution had strongly influenced the Assembly's decision. Moreover, could one trust decisions that could be abolished at any given moment? Hadn't Sonthonax declared the abolition of slavery in 1793, a last recourse in attempting to save the French colony by obtaining the support of slaves and their leaders? And what was this expedition doing ten years later? Weren't they saying that they'd come to reinstate slavery?

Several weeks later, Jérôme left the French Army and joined the Indigenous Army. Three of the blacks from the unit came with him; the other blacks were executed for treason.

Since childhood, Cécile had wanted to plan everything. Angeline would make fun of her when she persisted in organizing the most minute details of their childhood games, giving instructions and orders on who was doing what and when. As an adult, Cécile planned her life in the service of her vision of the world and of other people. And here she was immersed in the present moment with an intensity that nullified any notion of past and future. She obeyed her desires without questioning them. Each meeting, each embrace seemed to be both the beginning and the end, the conclusion and the quest; she returned satisfied, thirsty, already anxious about being at the next encounter.

A week went by before their second meeting; it was a week during which Cécile had tried to forget the intensity she felt when Amédée's hand had brushed against her skin for a mere second. Was it by mistake or was it simply because it had to be? An unknown force was pushing them toward each other. She had wanted to erase the burn that his eyes had left on her breasts, the bite felt just by looking at his lips. She hadn't known that she was harboring so much fervor within—a moist and wild warmth that he had unleashed in one look.

The morning of the seventh day, she gave up the struggle, for no other reason than the unspeakable desire to see him again, to savor his skin, to press her body against his, and to let passion consume her completely. He saw her approach him, unreserved, and took her hand without guile. He welcomed her without comment, as if her anticipated departure, her helpless look, and her skirt held by a nervous hand had foretold her reappearance.

At first, she tried, if not to hide, at least not to display her relationship with Amédée so as not to hurt her parents. But when the desire to see him overtook her, she forgot social conventions and prejudices. The need to be with him swept away all the hesitations. Of course, she imagined and feared the reactions of her family. Esther and Georges Lespinasse would be devastated by the thought of their only daughter compromising herself with this African lover, whose feet were firmly planted in the dusty roads, his arms tattooed with the scars of servitude and revolt, his somber gaze that of one who had nothing to lose. She herself had to admit that she would never have thought to embark on this adventure with such abandon. But the war had changed her mind, made her more able to make the most of each moment and not let herself be limited by the expectations of others. She had always been quick to rebel, but always within acceptable limits. For the first time, she realized that she'd crossed the point of no return, but she couldn't bring herself to worry about it.

He also seemed to want to take in life by big gulps, and so whenever possible they'd meet: in the city, in the market, on street corners, next to the fountain. Boldly, he once came as far as her father's shop to get her, exactly on the day they were wrapping up fabric to bring it back home since Georges Lespinasse had decided to close the shop. When he saw his daughter conversing with this tall negro with a wild look about him, he closed the door violently.

She would go to find him at the camp, where they accepted her numerous visits with smiles and mocking laughter, given that she was Angeline's friend and an informant. She sought him in the fields, by the streams, by the water—he was everywhere she directed her gaze—and life amounted to the mixing of their sweat, to their interlocking legs, to their bellies pressed against each other, and to the cries and sighs that could never fully express the need that gnawed at them constantly.

She didn't dare ask herself if she would have followed Amédée under different circumstances. She suspected that this relationship wouldn't survive the war, but who among them would survive? How could one predict the future? Meanwhile, she delighted in the burning harmony of their bodies, in the instinctive complicity of their gestures, and in the pleasure that they shared with each other, so easily, so intensively. The urgency of the clashes, the intensity of the violence surrounding them. gave their embraces a desperate taste that made them even more irresistible.

At the beginning, Ferdinand himself, the incorrigible libertine, had tried, weakly and under parental pressure, to dissuade her from continuing to be seen with this man. Then unambiguously one day he began to urge her to be happy: "Go ahead, little sister, enjoy your life."

A short while later, Cécile learned that the mulatto woman Emma, Ferdinand's friend, had died of yellow fever. Many people from the city of Au Cap were still dying from it, and although most of them were French officers, some civilians had also perished. Cécile personally knew a dozen of them, even though the epidemic had waned. To avoid panic in the army's ranks, it was rumored, the French would gather corpses at night and throw them into the sea. But how did they hide from the other soldiers the losses in the sparse ranks, the absences, the personal belongings that no one claimed, the last breath lost in silence? Cécile volunteered to help those wounded in the rebels' camp by bringing them food and clothing, in support of the affected families. Possessing neither talent nor aptitude for cooking, she didn't venture to make food, but in the Lespinasse shop, despite her father's mumblings, she made caracos, fashionable fitted jackets for women, out of scraps from more or less matching fabric.

One day she noticed Désirée in full color, as usual, but with her hair undone and her skirt torn. Cécile thought that she had to have been assaulted by a soldier or by one or more of them and wanted to go to her, but the young woman disappeared at a corner of a road, and Cécile wasn't able to follow her tracks.

She asked here and there for news about Désirée, but no one had seen her recently. Cécile thought that she must have joined one of the rebel groups, and became worried. How was she going to survive? Who would protect her? Was she with her adoptive brother? Cécile told herself that surely the young woman in full color was managing, and that there was no reason to worry; that imminent death added anxiety to the most banal actions.

Anguish lived on in her, anyway. The troops were preparing for the decisive battle, and she was afraid for her family, her friends, for Angeline in particular, for her Uncle Pierre, for Amédée, Désirée, and all those whose paths she'd crossed. She would have wanted to eliminate the clashes, but she knew that at this stage war was inevitable.

Zinga tried in vain to calm Désirée down. Carried away by desire, Zinga had wanted to lie on top of her. Motivated as well by concern for her protection, since the atmosphere was becoming more and more filled with echoes from the war: shellfire, shots, screams, the noise of boots. He wanted to know she was safe, under the protection of his own body. It was an enormous mistake, and he knew it as soon as he saw her widened eyes and mouth forming an expression of terror and rage. He was too late. He rolled to the side, but she was already attacking him with her nails, throwing herself on top of him, unleashing a fury that increased her strength tenfold. Obviously, with a few moves he could have immobilized her, but being too overwhelmed by the insanity he saw in her eyes, he was content to cover his eyes with his hands to avoid her scratches.

Désirée's airy voice had always seemed sensual to him, and he loved hearing her purring with pleasure when his fingers traced the outline of her body, discovering its essence and returning it to her to taste. But on that day, he didn't recognize the tone of the furious adolescent who was insulting him in an outpouring, spewing from a malfunctioning spinning top, with words like "soft-balled bastard," and "cursed whitey," and "rapist's son" coming back at him. Finally, he had to hold her in his arms to avoid her punching fists and her feet kicking in all directions.

"I'm sorry, it's me. It's me," he repeated in the hollow of her ear. He listened to her screams diminish then finally stop. With her eyes still dry but less wild, he sensed that she was once again ready to pounce, but he dared to lift and embrace her. He headed in the direction of the sea, which had the power to console her. He'd have brought her to the end of the other world if he could. The thought of having almost lost her made him as weak as a baby goat.

He had never seen her cry. Even during nightmares that turned her body into a dangerous tornado that was frightening to watch, and from which she'd wake up soaked in memories that made her blood run cold—memories too heavy to bear—not a single tear came to her eyes. He would have preferred to see her burst into tears, maybe then an ounce or two of this terrible burden would leave her. But no. She kept her eyes strangely dry and would let escape from her lips the slight cries of a wounded child.

He wondered what he should do to keep her protected. Would she accept staying far from the fighting? Did he have the right to ask her to clip her wings? She, who would climb trees to see the ocean? She, who would go completely naked into the water and who'd swim with such casualness that the waves would recede? Did he have the right to want to transform this bird-woman-swimmer into a calm and silent doll?

He, Zinga the African, the warrior who had decided long ago to fight no matter what came of it, to remain free—he got scared. Dark, menacing thoughts entered his mind and he felt a cold wind go through him.

The war was reaching its end. The French troops were getting tired. Between the continuous skirmishes, yellow fever, the heat, ticks, and all kinds of illnesses that they weren't used to, their numbers had decreased dramatically. It had been more than a year since the war ships had arrived, stocked full of weapons—these mouths of fire ready to devour negroes—so much blood had been shed. The French had tried to carry out their plan of getting rid of the black officers who were a grade higher than that of captain. This rumor had spread panic among the black officer ranks and caused several of them to desert. It had also intensified the black population's feeling that they had to fight to keep their threatened freedom.

Like so many others, Zinga was persuaded that the French troops had received the order not to back down no matter what so they could reinstate the old system. The dogs, bulldogs imported from Cuba, the torture, the drownings and the lynchings—all of this was proof. The French didn't hesitate to kill women and children.

What would they do if Désirée ever fell into their hands? The young woman's actions were often unexpected, obeying their own logic, often incomprehensible to others. Even faced with the rebel troops and the Indigenous Army, she was still in danger. Anything could happen.

Fear took him by the guts. Instinctively, Zinga embraced the young woman more, holding her against his body. She had fallen asleep, but from time to time, huge sobs shook her chest and the words of a fearful child escaped her lips.

Guillaume had rejoined the Indigenous Army almost two years ago, but Marie Nago's arrival in his life gave new meaning to his enlistment, a peaceful and determined one. He found in the young woman's gait a refreshing courage; she was always ready to let her laughter ring out, without an ounce of defeatism even in the face of the most difficult situations. Guillaume admired that even after having folded under the shock caused by the shards of retrieved memory, after having spent three days in deep solitude caused by the chaos of her mind, she had come out of it even stronger. He'd wanted to enter this wounded place with her, but he knew that she had to heal herself alone. He could only wait for her on the outside. When she emerged from her silence, she reclaimed everything: the past, the present, the years on the island living under a name imposed by their ledger. She had reappropriated the two names that absorbed one part of misfortune, one dose of tenderness, and the fate of indescribable moments that gave to each of them a different, unique scent. Standing tall in her dignity, with her pain wrapped in her closed fist, she mixed it all together: preserving, caressing, nourishing, washing, scrubbing, to reach for who she was now, always Akissi Marie Nago, in all her fullness.

Like her, Guillaume the Griffe had taken on his state of being to make of it an armor, a shield, a comforter in which he could nestle to protect himself from the blows that were too hard.

They both had to be strong to face the coming battle. The months and weeks were expected to be decisive and violent. Saint-Domingue had reached the point of no return, and the two parties were going to have to fight until the end. Guillaume rejoiced in the bravery and intelligence of the men of the Indigenous Army. At the very beginning of the year, he was assigned to La Tortue with one of the battalions of the Ninth Demi-Brigade. Their raids against the French and their resistance had earned them the reputation of brave men who never surrendered, who fought to the death. Guillaume the Griffe was proud to serve under the orders of General François Capois—the one who accepted no weakness. The first to throw himself in battle, without fear, without hesitation, the first to spur the others to action, the first to keep their courage and will strong and high. Guillaume had learned a great deal from his contact with this man, and he'd boast of being once again in his demi-brigade even while the fight was nearing its end.

Not only was Capois a soldier, a strategist capable of organizing and leading his troops, but he was fighting for an idea, affirming that the blacks were also human like everyone else.

"As black as we are," he'd say, "we have the same rights."

The men in his brigade would often repeat these words forcefully. Recently, they had taken the habit of calling him "Capois, the Death Man." Guillaume didn't really know why. All kinds of explanations were circulating, but Guillaume thought that it was simply because Capois was not afraid of dying. Nor was he the only one, in fact. Guillaume had seen it in the actions of those who were fighting at his side. The soldiers of the Indigenous Army went to combat without fear, as if death were part of the game and that they'd decided to play 'til the very end.

What happens when we realize that we've been only half a self? What happens when we realize that a large part has been tucked away in memory, or rather in oblivion? When one realizes that deep within oneself there was an immense clean wall that had been whitewashed, and when one passed one's hands over it, dust from nowhere would stick to one's fingers. When I started reconnecting to my previous life, I remained in a vegetative state for a few days during which the voices outside couldn't reach me. I was in a whirlwind where out-of-focus images, confusing odors, an unusual swarming on my skin were making a torturous path, simultaneously painful and luminous, into my memory. There were figures of children whose smiles suddenly resonated in me, shapes of animals whose names returned with a sense of recognition that burned my lips, the music of a known language that my ears remembered. Images would bring whiffs of odors; the aromas came with an avalanche of emotions that awakened all my senses. Along with my mother's face, the horror also returned. I experienced the pain of the capture and the crossing, the crush, my child's panic in this inhuman upheaval, my hands clutching my mother's dress, my tears joining those of others around me. I know the fear of darkness, the darkness of the ship's hold at night, when the bodies pressed one against another would sleep with no escape from nightmares. I remember the anger and the revolt. I hear bodies being thrown overboard, or ones that throw themselves into the waters. When I emerged from this unspeakable backwash, I felt submerged in colors, in fragrances, in words. My skin felt different, my body seemed to be a strange place that I needed to rediscover. In looking at my face, I detected sudden resemblances with other faces and the stench of other bodies on my skin. When I reached the surface with the weight of my nine years of age before the time of the ship ledgers cupped in my hands, I looked at this land that I'd learned to love, the trees, the mountains, the currents, the sea at the end of the familiar horizon, the grass beneath my feet, and I felt as new as the hills washed by the rain at dawn. See, I looked at this earth with my eyes wide open, full of images and memories, and still loved her: with my bare eyes, I loved her more than ever. Guillaume the Griffe had called me his flame tree, "beautiful and strong with flowers in her hair." This land was a part of me, and I could only love her in order not to break the branches of this tree that I had become.

After this plunge into my childhood, I threw myself into the fight with even more zeal. To take into account what I had experienced gave me more strength, adding to the strength of the other young people, women and men who like me had been forced to change places, to resign themselves to their fate, to give up on what they were leaving behind. Those, like me, who had to fight to not be buried alive in this new world that they had to reinvent while they were rewriting their history, as I am rewriting mine. Holding my past in my right hand, and my present in my left hand, and my forehead facing straight ahead.

Moussa had assigned my group the task of being scouts, a position that held special risks. We weren't directly fighting the enemy, but it was possible to encounter a bigger and better equipped troop and not be able to defend ourselves, since we didn't have the same weapons. Until now we'd been lucky and everything was going well. The battle in Crête-à-Pierrot taught me a lot. First, do not underestimate the enemy and always have an exit strategy, but especially remember that the will to fight must always remain in us. Each person had to muster their strength. Some used their religious beliefs as a ramp, and they seemed fearless, without any fear of dying. The *lwa* from Ginen were accompanying them, guiding them, and death for them was merely a return from where they had come originally. For others, it was rage and anger that gave them the strength to move their feet and agitate their arms. And as for me, I clung to my love of life to keep me from giving up, and not to hesitate when action and moving forward were necessary—even when death was waiting around the corner. I loved life too much to accept that metal chains, regulations enforced with the end of a whip, or laws written on stamped paper could break me. Living under these conditions meant dying slowly, and I preferred a big wood fire in which I'd go up in smoke rather than see myself disappear among miserable little twigs.

We had already lost everything when they captured us, wrenching us away from our homes to bring us here. We fought to get this semblance of freedom that they were now threatening to take away. So we had nothing to lose, but in fact we had everything to gain in this fight. It was as simple as that. Our laughter would ring out, which scared the whites; they looked at each other, taken aback when they heard us, not knowing whether they should attribute it to insanity, naïveté, and carefreeness or to a courage that went above and beyond human capacity. And this scared the wits out of them; embarrassed by the discomfort caused by the laughter, they didn't dare turn their eyes in our direction. Some people made the sign of the cross, others took their bayonets and their rifles, aiming everywhere as if they were hysterics incapable of controlling the panic that was overcoming them. Guillaume told me that he overheard one of them whisper, "It's the devil laughing," and the others had quickly made the sign of the cross and mumbled prayers to their God.

I hadn't seen Désirée again for several days, so I naturally looked for her. My eyes searched for bright colors, the quick almost imperceptible movement of her long legs. I had caught a glimpse of her when she was with the tall African man who seemed to want to keep her, like the gold stolen by the Spaniards from the island's first inhabitants. The elders often spoke of this stolen treasure as if it gave them even more reason to fight, because nothing or no one would protect us on this land. But the little one wasn't the kind to be enclosed in a dome or in any kind of cage, whether it was golden or not. It's hard to trap a butterfly without hurting its wings, without marring its beauty.

I wanted to tell her at least to be careful, not to go near Boulet's plantation. Rumors were that the planter was looking to take revenge for everything that was happening around him, for his gambling losses, for the most recent mistress—a quadroon who'd left him for her lover, an Ibo man. His friend Martineau had left the island, and Boulet was regretting having waited too long to decide. Boulet had gathered some armed men and was being vindictive and cruel, especially toward his former slaves. Désirée's name would sometimes cross his lips with a sneer that foretold nothing good. Guillaume also didn't want his sister to go near the ramparts or Fort Picolet. She loved to lean out there on her elbows and look at the ocean. We noticed how she'd become more and more nervous, and we were afraid of her reactions to the scenes of war. What would happen in this deadly brouhaha? I had promised Guillaume to try and stay close to her and protect her in case she became agitated. War was intensifying emotions. Désirée, who was more sensitive than others, had become like a palm leaf detached from a tree and tossed around at the whim of the wind. Any vicious puff could set her adrift.

Cécile's life had moved so far away from anything she could have imagined that she wondered if she was dreaming. She would never have thought she'd feel so fulfilled at times, while the war continued wreaking its inevitable havoc. Never could she have imagined Au Cap in such a state of ruin and desolation. Cécile no longer recognized the city in which she had been born and had grown up so well surrounded and protected. Some streets were strewn with debris, remnants of skirmishes and battles, some houses had damaged doors and walls, the shutters gaping, revealing glimpses of interiors where life seemed missing. It's true that last year's fire had left its traces, even if the houses had since been rebuilt. But what made the city so desolate was not just the fire that Christophe had set in the face of the aggression of Leclerc and the French troops, it was the emptiness. So many people had deserted the city! The planters left in great numbers and boarded ships headed for France. Others took refuge in the abandoned ships as they waited to depart. For the people of color and the free blacks, it was less obvious. Most of them clung to this land, their birthplace, not only to the city but to the entire island. How to leave? Where to go? What else could they do but fight to remain free, even if their hearts clenched at the thought of such carnage? Several of the Lespinasse family's friends had fled the city to take refuge up in the hills or farther out in the countryside. After much deliberation, Cécile's parents had decided to follow them as soon as the shop was closed. Uncle Emmanuel had welcomed his family without hesitation. The Lespinasses stuck together. Obviously glad to be in a situation where they were in control, though it was relative and temporary, Uncle Emmanuel "suggested" to Ferdinand and Cécile that they not go into town to avoid being assaulted or attacked. Despite her tendency to protest, the young woman had to admit that on top of the risks they incurred, it hurt her to see her city in this state. Passing by the embankments filled her with sadness. Empty and dirty, they looked miserable in contrast to the opulent spectacle and intense comings and goings that used to define them. No ships, or very few, were drawn alongside the quays since the English blockade had begun last July. The trestles that the farmers set up to sell their garden produce were no longer lined up along the avenue. There were no wheelbarrows, no carts filled with merchandise on their way to the shops. In fact, most of the shops were closed and a food shortage was threatening the city. The people were in dire straits, even beyond the supplies that were lacking, and the fear of falling victim to the violence was reflected in their eyes. Now without a doubt, the war was here. And the city of Cap-Français was at the center of it.

Cécile wasn't deluding herself about the situation, but despite it all, a profound happiness possessed her. Her meetings with Amédée satisfied her physically and helped her discover her own body—this body that she had always considered less important than her intellectual prowess. Since meeting Amédée, she saw herself differently. Her body was wholly present, rooted in her happiness. Each part of her body, each piece of her skin lived with an intensity that she avidly absorbed. She would have liked to be able to share this joy with Angeline, to talk with her of this experience about which they had both dreamed, but her friend was enclosed in her own fierce and somber world and received her attempts at communication with a restraint that hurt Cécile. She missed her friend's lively and exuberant intelligence. She missed her friendship.

Despite her sadness at seeing Angeline change, Cécile understood Angeline's need to avenge her brothers. She also shared her frustrations and her anguish in the face of an uncertain future. In one of their last private conversations, Angeline had brought up the reinstatement of slavery in Guadeloupe by the French. "Who knows what they want to do here? And if they reinstate it here, you think they won't question our status as free blacks, and even the status of people of color!?" Other people had reached the same conclusions. They all had to unite—the victory would be for everyone.

Cécile, however, had decided not to join the ranks. The active scene that she found in the camp of the Army of the Incas, which became known as the Indigenous Army, was enormously appealing to her. But her worry about her parents was stronger than her desire to join the troops. Over the month of July, her father had fallen ill, which the doctor attributed to the concerns and worries caused by the situation: the closure of the shop, the move to Uncle Emmanuel's house, and the city's general ambience. This illness left him weakened and sullen. Cécile couldn't forget her mother's eyes when they last met. Sad but proud, full of dignity but with a hint of vulnerability that suddenly made Cécile realize that her parents were becoming old. Her cousins, Uncle Emmanuel's sons, had signed up a few months before Ferdinand. Cécile decided therefore that her presence in Haut-Limbé was necessary, at least until things calmed down. If they ever calmed down . . .

She had told herself that in the meantime, she could help in other ways. So, every week she brought clothes for the officers and soldiers who needed them. Some men were practically in rags, others were wearing uniforms that were patched up. Shoes were needed, and sometimes food as well. It broke her heart to see the deplorable conditions in which the indigenous troops were operating, but Cécile thought that the situation was undoubtedly worse for the French troops. They couldn't count on the local population's support. When they didn't receive their ration of often rotten biscuits, the soldiers would go so far as to eat rats, devour grass and leaves.

Though generally not very talkative, Amédée had told Cécile about the only time that his gang had spared an enemy troop. He'd seen this French battalion going at a baby goat that they roasted on a makeshift fire. Their hunger was so strong that they couldn't wait. He saw them eat the half-raw meat. They were fighting among themselves, like savages, for bits of flesh. His troop could have easily disarmed them. They were a bunch of poor fellows, Poles who didn't know what they were doing in the colony, still overwhelmed by the enormity of their experiences since their arrival. To keep this colony that had given it so much, France had sent soldiers of all kinds. Many young men lost their lives here without knowing why. The troop let the eleven soldiers go, but they confiscated what remained of the meat and grilled it with hot peppers and spices. Amédée roared with laughter, just thinking about it. Then he immediately resumed a gloomy expression. He refused to lie about the fate that the Indigenous Army reserved most of the time for their enemies. "Normally, we execute them. We expect them to kill us, too, if we're captured. This is war and there's no pity for the enemy."

Despite the horror she felt, Cécile thought she had no right to judge those who had suffered more than she had from slavery and the brutality of the former colonizers, and who now found themselves fighting the French Army. War could not happen without violence, and no side could back down.

The young woman sighed as she imagined the fate of her friends and acquaintances who had joined the ranks of the Indigenous Army, if they were ever injured. Of course, the sick and the wounded benefited from the care of the healers and a few rare doctors who accompanied some units, but if the wounds were serious, it would be fatal. The healers couldn't manage big emergencies. She knew the state of the two main hospitals in the city, the Providence Hospital and the Hospital of the Fathers, which besides didn't treat blacks. One of Uncle Emmanuel's former workhouse laborers who cleaned the Hospital of the Fathers had described the horrors that occurred there. The soldiers, the doctors themselves, were dying, corpses were piling up. An odor of rot, of rotting carcasses, met visitors. The wounded who were brought to the hospital would die in a matter of days, sometimes hardly a day later. Given that there weren't enough beds, the sick and the wounded would sometimes be two in a bed. Rats and other vermin would crawl out of the cracks in the wall. Infections spread quickly. The lack of materials, equipment, and medicine was evident in the unbearable stench and the indescribable chaos.

Cécile shuddered at the thought of her friend, the beautiful Angeline, or even Ferdinand being in such a place. Her brother's decision to enlist provoked rather unexpected reactions in the family. Except for a sigh and a sign of the cross, heavy and slow like an act of contrition, their mother didn't show her anguish, which was unusual. The news had apparently affected Georges Lespinasse a great deal more; he'd repeated, like a leitmotiv: "What did he say? What did he say?" Cécile detected a hint of surprised pride in his voice.

The young woman had managed to hide her own surprise when her brother announced his decision to her. "Death spares no one," he whispered, "so it's better to face it squarely. I have nothing to lose and have enough anger in me to become a good soldier!"

It saddened Cécile to see, under a layer of his typical cynicism, this raw pain in Ferdinand's eyes. She who had so often wished that her brother's immense intelligence be used for something other than hatching plans to collect female conquests, today she wondered, what right did she have to think that she could judge the importance of things, deciding what mattered and what didn't matter? The war had turned everything upside down.

However, maybe the war wasn't a reality to everyone. Friends had told her that there were still dances taking place in town, and there were still performances of plays by famous French authors. Yet barely a few feet away, women and men who were merely skin and bones were waiting to die.

Ma Aza, why did you leave me? I know you didn't want to, but I feel lost without you. I told the children. Gilles and Virginie cried, Fatima giggled stupidly. I fear for her and I'm also afraid of her sometimes. The city has changed, even the woods have changed. I hear sounds that don't come from either animals, or trees, or the river. Men have taken over the woods, and they have rifles and batons and machetes. There is so much noise and movement. The animals are afraid, and the birds have flown up to the highest branches.

It's true, Désirée, there's too much noise around here. I want to go find my mother.

Me too, I want to go find Caleb. There's blood everywhere.

Children, Ma Aza is no longer here. I want us to stay together to protect each other.

It's time to grow up, Désirée, my love. Look at me, I'll never be as tall or as beautiful. I'm fixed in time, in this blue dress that I loved so much. This blue dress stained with blood.

What are you saying? Children, be quiet. Stay. Zinga will be here soon, and he'll protect us from everything.

Zinga doesn't know we exist. He only sees you. In fact, where was your Zinga this morning? Those men were going to hurt you. You see how your skirt is torn, they almost caught you. The world is full of evil people, you must defend yourself.

I don't want you to leave, I don't want to be alone. Let's go look for Zinga. We must find him. He'll know what to do.

Too much noise, Désirée. I don't want to stay here. I'm tired, I want my mother.

Ma Aza has left. Don't leave me alone, children.

She's dead, Désirée. Ma Aza has died. Face the truth. She has died. We are dead.

The little one is right. Too much noise, Désirée. Where's Caleb?

Go ahead, tell her where Caleb is, Désirée. You want to keep them forever. Look around you. It's war. It's the end. You must decide.

I'm going to look for Zinga, Guillaume, and Marie Nago. They'll know what to do.

When she returned to the plains of Cul de Sac, our friend Elsa yelled, "Marie Nago, Bayi, come see!" Proudly, she then showed a piece of blue and red fabric like a trophy; then after endless discussion, it was placed in a cotton sack. Sometimes, someone from the group will pull it out to show it to other insurgents. I couldn't stop myself from sighing from happiness and pride each time I saw it.

Yet I had become accustomed to seeing flags flying. Spanish flags, English flags, and especially the French ones: on the mast of the ships that brought us here, on those that brought merchandise from the metropole, or those that were filled with coffee, cotton, sugar, and spices before the sail was lifted. I had seen the French flag flying atop their desks, at the gendarmerie, in all these places where their laws were applied against us, against our condition as human beings. I had seen it showcase its colors—blue, white, red—taunting our efforts, our struggles, our suffering.

The general-in-chief's headquarters were located in the Petite-Rivière of Artibonite. Elsa was telling us that's where he commanded one of his men to remove the white strip from the tricolored French flag. At first, none of them, including her, understood right away what he wanted to do. Was it an act of defiance against France? Was it an angry gesture? Was it an affront to the symbol that had accompanied all the French actions against the Indigenous Army troops? Then, Dessalines tied the two remaining strips and waved them very high. And without a command and in perfect harmony, the soldiers saluted the new indigenous flag. From that point on, I saw the groups post other flags: some red ones, some red and black ones—and I saluted them with equal pride and fervor. We created these flags, we chose them. Some people grumbled that they were just strips of fabric, that we shouldn't make a big deal out of them. It was probably true but many of us no longer wanted to see the flags flown on the masthead of ships that had brought us here. The flags belonging to those who had kept us captive, condemned to suffer for their benefit. The strips of fabric themselves could also tell other stories: stories of blue skies, stories of blood, stories of victory.

Others remembered that Dessalines didn't always understand the interests of the cultivators; and at one time, he had carried out Leclerc's repressive orders. Truth be told, I didn't understand why Christophe, Dessalines, and Pétion had remained faithful to the orders given by Rochambeau's army. Moussa often complained that the officers' strategy had sacrificed many African chiefs who were fighting for freedom, while they were the ones who sustained the revolt and gathered the cultivators. The black military leaders should have rallied around the African leaders from the beginning. Guillaume confided in me that some of his comrades told him how the French officers pitted the blacks against the mulattoes. "A game of the duped, since mulattoes also used the blacks against the whites, and the blacks caught in between would often make fun of both groups." Often, too, the behavior of the white officers angered the mulattoes who were in solidarity with the blacks. It was a real mix-up whereby, from one day to the next, one group would take the place of another.

I was relieved when all the black generals had finally withdrawn from the French Army. Dessalines was now the general-in-chief of the Indigenous Army, which united blacks and mulattoes. Manipulation was over, at least for now. I had become cautious, but I didn't want to lose hope despite the growing number of losses. My only consolation was that from the French side it was worse. But how could we account for the deaths of friends like we would for bags of coffee that we'd load on a ship? Each loss came with its portion of pain, and even if the loss receded for a moment in the heat of military action, it remained in the shadows waiting for the moment when it would remind us that a friend was no longer with us.

Moussa had returned from the last battle with one less arm. To avoid gangrene, they'd had to amputate his arm. We all avoided looking at him at first, but he simply began to train even more than he had before. For days, I saw him wake up even earlier than usual, drawing the baton with his right hand against Master Silo, and then he'd take the bayonet and practice using it with one hand. He took up leading the group again, and all of us had saluted him the way one would salute a chief who is respected and admired. Guillaume had talked to me about his general François Capois, who was such a courageous and decent man that he was called "Capois, the Death Man." As for me, I had no nicknames to give to Moussa, to the men and women fighting alongside me. But I knew that their courage was feeding my own, that the occasional peals of laughter gave me strength and confidence, that when we walked together to face the enemy, our courage became a beam that lit our path. We depended on each other. We were together, united to fight, in life, and, if necessary, until death.

Zinga, silent, was looking at the hills that surrounded him. It did him good to take a little breather, but he couldn't linger long. He had to get ahead of the enemy and didn't want to lose a single soldier. In this war, it was almost impossible not to incur losses, but each time someone in his group fell, a mixture of rage and sadness would come over him. It wasn't only for those in his group, but for all those lives which passed in this way, some who hadn't yet reached the milestone of twenty years of age.

Around him, the mountains towered as always, majestic. The fog seemed to hide behind them, like a gossamer scarf that the wind would twirl playfully. How far away it seemed from the time when he'd look at this landscape with detachment and resentment!

The enemy troops were advancing, and he gave the order to continue on course. He was proud of these men and women who charged with courage, who talked, got angry, laughed, but would never imagine surrendering. He had come to know them, to recognize the extraordinary strength of Maki, the efficient strategist in Marie-Anne, the bravery behind Sayira's placid smile, the infallible Mahmoud's insight, Samson's discreet ability to lift spirits when the morale of some of them wavered. Sleeping together under the stars, wiping away the first drops of dew, all of them feeling the pangs of hunger and thirst, seeing together the enemy troops withdraw, facing death, escaping together—this forged a bond so strong that nothing could separate them. His group had become a closely knit unit that acted in perfect harmony, a solidarity on which he could depend. Almost all were African, starting from those who had arrived on the last slave ships, who hadn't had the time or who refused, as Zinga had done, to acclimate to the new place, customs, language. To those considered *bossales,* as if all of them should have accepted the conditions of their new life. In the groups of rebels, there were so many more like them. Zinga knew that without the Africans the fight could not have spread so rapidly. Without them, would there have been this tidal wave to wash over the entire colony from all sides? News came about the battles in the South and in the center. Africans were present everywhere, and no one could cast any doubt on their knowhow and courage. Yet, Zinga the African was afraid for his companions, not only for death, which was constantly lurking, but also for the future, after the war. Could they break themselves free from the horrors and indignities they'd suffered to cling to their dreams as human beings and not stumble? Anger and shame weigh so much. And especially, what would postbattle Saint-Domingue offer them? Would they be treated as equal men and women, they who claimed not only the right to be free but also the right to have free access to the land?

Zinga advanced in long strides, hurried but sure and measured. On the alert, all his senses guided his steps. Yet he didn't stop thinking about Désirée. He hadn't seen her since he'd left her in a small creek after their last encounter. Hoping that she'd be protected in that calmer site, since it was close to the sea, but knowing very well that no one could predict Désirée's actions.

He had asked his group to leave instructions warning her, in case anyone saw her. But in the heat of action, in the face of danger, how does one ask combatants to pay attention to a young woman who skipped like a gazelle and who seemed to fly like a bird—a young woman with sad eyes who smiled while chattering in a child's voice, or who would sob without ever shedding tears?

Zinga sighed. He couldn't rid himself of the anguished weight that had followed him since the last time he saw Désirée. It was as if tragedy awaited them. But maybe only one of them was threatened? Which one, then? Was it he? He, who only believed in the powers down here? He, who mistrusted instinctively all ideas that interpreted human behavior through a supernatural lens? He suddenly became scared of this premonition that lingered within him.

Fatima! What are you doing? Be careful, please. Here, it's like during the big ceremony where the fire made the men dance and where the women threw themselves onto the ground, while the animals screeched and the leaves of the trees whispered. I couldn't understand what they were saying to each other. Today, you hear the drums in your head, but it's the blood of animals that's flowing, it's the blood of men and women. So much blood. Fatima! I'm scared.

Yes, I know you're afraid, Désirée. Gilles and Virginie are hidden—I see them, but I don't hear them. It's always like this when you're afraid, they go into hiding. But you, you can't hide, can you?

You understood nothing. I don't want to hide, Fatima. Guillaume is in battle, my little brother is fighting somewhere and he might get hurt. Marie Nago is also fighting. She's the one who likes to laugh. Really laugh, unlike me. When I laugh my heart cries, but when she laughs, Marie Nago's eyes sparkle, her heart dances, and I'd love to be able to laugh like her. One day.

You can always dream, Désirée. Your heart aches, yet you can't cry.

I'm looking for Zinga too, he must be in the heat of battle. I'm afraid for him, I'm afraid for Guillaume, Marie Nago, Zinga, Cécile—that girl who wanted to make me a dress of many colors—I'm scared for us. I don't know why but I feel like I have to find Zinga soon. But he must be careful. I don't want us to be caught.

Me, I'm not afraid, and I'm going to charge ahead—it's what you do when facing the enemy. If only I had done it that day . . .

You're not responsible for what these two vultures did to you that day. And then today, you see how you responded when faced with this white soldier who wanted to catch us. You pelted his face with stones. He dropped his weapons to protect his face.

Anyway, I'm not afraid. Don't worry about me. Nothing worse can happen to me, my little one.

I had physically prepared myself for battle. My already hardened body had chosen to train without a break, my reflexes with the baton and the machete had become refined—so much so that Master Silo gave me a real compliment. "Great job, little Marie." Every day, I brought on the battlefield this precious gift as if it were a talisman.

Under Moussa's command, my companions and I were camouflaged in the hills behind the city, near Charrier. We had to prevent all attempts to bring reinforcements to the French troops. For five days, we were on the lookout and our excitement was rising. We knew that the general-in-chief had ordered the capture of Vertières. On their side, the Indigenous Army's troops were getting ready. Guillaume, who was once again in Capois's brigade, was going to be on the front lines. From time to time, my body wanted to split and go find him where he was. The day before, I had overheard old Lola talking about people who were able to teleport themselves elsewhere when necessary. It seems that from Plaisance, a father had been able to go to Au Cap to get medicine that the doctor had prescribed to save his son's life. According to what Ma Lola was saying, the trip took him only two hours. I would have loved to have this power and to slip next to Guillaume, if only for one second, to press against him to protect him and feel the heat of his body. But for the survival of all of us, my *bon anj* must remain alert and vigilant, while the faithful and favorable images of my man washed over me, to keep me company without agitating me.

The sixth day of our mission, the scouts laughed once, then a second time. The rustling of leaves, the sounds of muffled steps, the smell of wet grass were spreading more because the ground had been disturbed in its previously calm state. The laughter returned. The alert was sounded. A troop of about thirty French soldiers approached. Despite their tired faces, they fought with the strength of despair, knowing in advance that they'd be vanquished. From our perspective, we knew that the Battle of Vertières would be decisive, so our courage grew. Bayi, who had joined Moussa's group a few months ago, was fighting with three or four French soldiers. But I couldn't do anything to support her, because facing me was a fierce man with enraged eyes. I managed to strike him in the chest with the machete and rushed to help out my other comrades. I could no longer glimpse Bayi. When it was over, Moussa, who'd become even more fearless since he'd become one-armed, quickly sized up the scene. We had a dozen prisoners and had lost ten companions. Moussa ordered the burial of our comrades and the collecting of the French corpses. We had already confiscated the weapons of the enemy soldiers, who increased the number of prisoners for the Indigenous Army. Some of them would be executed, others would be spared if they could be of use to us.

Arriving at Vertières, Guillaume felt tall and proud. Like all the members of the Indigenous Army, he knew that this was the place where General Henri Christophe had told Bonaparte's French expedition that they wouldn't be able to enter the city. And indeed, Christophe had burned down Cap-Français rather than relinquish it. Was it a declaration of war or a confirmation of a war declared by the French with the arrival of the expedition? Was it a foregone conclusion of a crisis that had lasted for so many years? Guillaume looked around him and sighed as he faced the cruel weight of human actions.

The struggle would be difficult and decisive. As the general-in-chief had said, the army victorious at the Battle of Vertières would control the city of Au Cap.

Guillaume the Griffe fought with fury like so many others because he no longer wanted to live in indignity. They had to win. Around him, so many examples of bravery were spread out around him that it seemed perfectly normal to face death, to let danger know that freedom and the right to exist in dignity justified all risks.

Marie Nago's image beamed at him while he was dodging the pointed ends of bayonets, shooting his rifle and shouting, giving slaps of encouragement to his comrades, and receiving some too. Meeting her had shone a bright light on every phase of his life—bringing colors both vibrant and tender for which he yearned. Hers was a steadier light than Désirée's. Between two feints, the memory of Ma Aza and Ma Bashira also came to mind. The enemy was striking hard and he was going to respond without fail, but the images of those he loved were keeping him company, feeding this fire that was lying quiet within him. After the battle, he'd like to remember this pinewood fire that smelled of majestic and proud trees—a fire that was peaceful and strong, created with outstretched hands all reaching for the same victory. He knew he would need human warmth for the next battle. Whatever its end, the story had only just begun.

Under my headscarf, my hair was dripping wet. Rain had been falling for so long that I paid almost no attention to the raindrops and would mechanically swipe them away to see better. We were getting close to Vertières, but it wasn't an easy task. On the way, we sometimes had to face groups of French troops who were undoubtedly going to lend a hand to their own. We were still far from the fort when I saw Désirée. I was so relieved at the sight of her that I didn't notice that her clothes looked untidy, they were wet and sticking to her body. Even if her clothes were colorful and fanciful most of the time, the little one's clothes had always been clean, not torn and dirty as I saw them on that day. Her face was emaciated, it seemed to be close to disappearing because of its absent look. Her eyes stared at me, but I felt like they didn't see me. Where had she come from? She was rubbing her hands on her tattered skirt and skipping in a jerky way that brought to mind the gait of a bird with broken feet. I got close to her and tried to talk to her, but she ignored me—casting looks to the right and left as if she were searching for someone.

I lost the little one from sight because another group of Frenchmen were getting close, and they were followed by a battalion of the Indigenous Army. The brouhaha was such that we were fighting almost hand to hand, with someone's elbow against someone else's chest, bayonets and sabers colliding. The rifles shot, the batons, the machetes, were flying in all directions. I had a rifle, taken from the last prisoners, and I made use of it.

I only saw Désirée two days later. I had gone back up to the camp to keep Abdul company; he was completely crushed. Bayi had killed a good number of enemy soldiers before succumbing to grapeshot fire. Her death had broken Abdul, even physically his body seemed broken—it was that day that I learned from him that my friend Bayi had been expecting a baby. She wanted her pregnancy to be more advanced before telling me and Elsa. I tried to console Abdul, who was overtaken with sadness under the weight of this double loss, but I couldn't conjure up my friend Bayi's face without feeling my own sadness well up to the surface. We stayed side by side for a long time, silent and immobile as if to give pain time to become a part of us, time to teach us to accept it a little. My eyes were red and my head heavy from crying so much when I saw Désirée enter the camp's enclosure. I rushed toward her because her clothes were covered in blood. At first, I thought it was her own blood, but I understood right away that despite her red-stained skirt and her deep agitation, she was not wounded. She was brandishing a baton, ready and even wanting to attack. She lay into one of the guards, who under the threat of her menacing behavior, tried to block her way. She got free and landed a blow of her baton on his shoulder, executing perfectly one of Master Silo's favorite strikes. With a sudden move, I stopped her next blow and grabbed her waist from behind. She struggled with her feet and hands. I turned her toward me and shuddered as I faced her crazed look and the pitiful screams that were escaping her mouth. I didn't recognize this altered face that had seemed to have aged several years. A bitter grimace twisted her lips. She continued to fidget furiously and I wondered if she could see me. Finally, I slapped her to make her stop. She shivered and looked at me, bewildered. "Désirée Congo. Désirée Congo," I repeated her name several times as if to bring her out of the nightmare in which she seemed to be imprisoned. "Désirée Congo, Désirée Congo," and when finally she turned her eyes to me, I told her: "It's me, Marie Nago. Do you recognize me?" She huddled up against me: "Zinga is dead. He's dead," she cried out and burst into tears.

I'm looking for Zinga, I'm also looking for Guillaume and Marie Nago. I'm afraid. I'm looking for Zinga because I had a bad dream. Zinga was covered in blood and he was on the ground. I don't see Guillaume, I don't see him anywhere.

Fatima, don't make fun of me. I'm telling you to be careful and to not make any noise. We must warn Zinga that he's in danger. We have to do it.

There is so much noise. Not the sounds of the leaves of the trees or the sound of the river gliding on stones. Nor is it the sound of the bird building his nest. Nor the stirring of the dust of the road lifted by the early morning wind. I know all these sounds and they never scare me. Me neither, I don't disturb them. I know them and they know me. But today I hear cruel steps, I hear rifles that bang together, I hear voices yelling orders, I hear fear, I hear death. Yes, it's the sound of death that I'm hearing. Death is blowing a cold wind. I hear it, I feel it, it's getting closer, it's already taken Ma Aza, Ma Bashira, and all the others. I don't want it to take Zinga. Where is Guillaume? Where is my brother?

No, Fatima, stay calm. Don't move. Yes, I see Zinga, but the French are coming around the back of Fort Magny. We should pass on the other side. We have to warn Zinga and his group, otherwise they will be massacred.

Fatima, you can't fight the French. I'm going to find Zinga and tell him. Stop, Fatima. No, Fatima, no . . . Let me go, you bunch of drooping mouths, you bunch of rapists, let me go, I'm telling you, or I will blind you. Zinga.

No, oh no, Zinga no, the blood, blood is everywhere. I had seen it, I knew it. Zinga!

I had changed a lot over the course of these past three years. The pain of other people affected me. Memories from long ago have imposed themselves on me, other lives have become linked to mine. It was a long chain of life that made me more vulnerable, but at the same time stronger. Sorrows and shared pleasures anchored me and allowed me to see even further ahead. Désirée Congo's distress hit me brutally and I did nothing to protect myself from it. I would only have wanted to spare her this suffering that had thrust her in my arms.

The next day, one of the members of his group told me how the tall African Zinga, the group leader, the uncompromising combatant for freedom, had lost his life. Zinga the African had arranged his men and placed himself in the front as usual. That's why when Fatir died, the rebels had chosen him as their new leader. His group trusted him, and Mahmoud, who described his last moments alive, hid his emotions by stuffing his pipe to scratch his throat from time to time. They had set up an ambush to block the road from the French Army troops who were trying to reconquer Fort Magny, which overlooks the Fort aux Dames. They were about to attack the French soldiers as planned when the screams reached them. There was a screaming child's voice, followed by an angry shout of a woman, Mahmoud told us. Zinga the African froze for an instant; he gave brief, quick orders to his second in command and rushed ahead. Three French soldiers were surrounding the young woman while a fourth restrained her. They were all sniggering because she was struggling and railing against them. That's when the rebels knew that the woman was Désirée. Zinga had already freed the woman and had pushed her back to protect her with his body. One of the French soldiers tried to catch her by the arm, and Zinga placed himself between him and Désirée. The musket hit him directly in the chest. I didn't bother asking

Mahmoud about the fate of the four French soldiers; I understood immediately on seeing the man's hardened, tight lips that they were executed on the spot.

I never knew Zinga the African. We crossed paths only one single time, but his loss weighed heavily on me. His name was added to the already too long list of the disappeared. And Désirée's prostrated figure and devastated face would constantly remind us of his death. She no longer skipped, her sweet, melancholy smile had disappeared, only her eyes had kept their immense sadness. I didn't know how to pull Désirée out of this grief in which she had sunk.

I tried to stay close to her as much as I could. I watched over her when she was asleep and sat next to her when she was still; she'd keep her eyes open, empty. Sometimes, I'd play with one of the colored handkerchiefs that she'd wrap around her hair or around her neck. Désirée Congo. I repeated this name she'd chosen and which linked us, me and her. Me, Marie Nago, who came from elsewhere and was deeply rooted in this new land; and her, Désirée Congo, born in Saint-Domingue but conceived over there, carrier of this African blood that connected us. Désirée Congo. I repeated this name to bring her spirit back into our world, this cruel world that had harmed her. How is it not understandable that she no longer wants to return here?

Sometimes, curled up in a ball like a child, Désirée appeared calm. At other times, sobs would shake her frail body. All the tears that had been held back for so long would come out then, in constant small streams. At times, she'd cry even in her sleep, shaking her head to fight against the horrific images that must have been haunting her. Her despair overwhelmed me. But I told myself, too, that with these tears maybe some of the accumulated suffering that had been devouring her for so long would drift away.

Sometime afterward, I decided to go up to Vertières. Désirée seemed less devastated and had begun again in her own way to communicate with those around her. I handed her over to Ma Lola, the healer. I had to get closer to the battle. Get closer to Guillaume. The rain that had begun more than two weeks earlier was not stopping, and the musty smell of wet clothes mixed with the smell of the wet earth, death, ashes, burnt flesh, fear and hatred.

When I was able to catch a glimpse of Guillaume, I let out with each breath the anguish that had made me feverish. He gestured with his hand but didn't move from his post. I also was longing to see the general of the brigade, François Capois, about whom he'd talked so much. I was telling myself that there must be some exaggeration in all the praise I'd heard of him. But when I saw him, I couldn't help but admire both his audaciousness and his courage. One would have thought he was two people because he moved with such speed and boldness. His voice reached all the way to me, and while I was passing the munitions I heard him shout, "Grenadiers, on the attack!" Tireless and brave. I understood the admiration that he aroused in his troops. To Guillaume, he was a hero—a true one, whose actions didn't obey any norms, and who gave those whom he met the impression that they'd been chosen for an unforgettable spectacle.

On the orders of François Capois, the Ninth Demi-Brigade attacked Vertières, where a few hundred French soldiers had gathered. The fight turned out to be difficult, but they'd expected that. The first assault resulted in a great number of our men falling. The second one too. The urgency of the action guided our moves. I worked with others to pass the ammunition, without minding the noise, the weapons, the bodies that were raining down on us. The French canons made the bodies fly, but Capois didn't back down. Attack! Grenadiers, attack! This shout galvanized our troops because it carried our hopes, our dreams, our wild desire to be free. *Sa ki mouri zafè a yo.* Whoever dies, too bad for them. When his horse fell under the strike of enemy fire, General Capois got up and rushed forward, shouting even louder, "Attack! Grenadiers, attack!" Even more soldiers followed him, forgetting the sounds of rifles, forgetting the murderous force of canons, forgetting that death was thundering around them, to witness only the final victory. Grenadiers, attack!

The war was nearing its end, and the last miles of the way are always the longest. We left many dead soldiers in Vertières, a thousand or more, and many wounded ones too. The smell of men and women's fresh blood will remain for a long time, undoubtedly. But I imagine that this place will also retain a spirit of freedom and courage. Around five in the afternoon, Vertières fell under our weapons. The Indigenous Army had won the battle.

In fact, we didn't know it yet, but we had won the war.

We had won the war, but when I saw, among the many bodies hit, Guillaume's body bathing in its own blood, I let my rifle fall. Nothing mattered anymore.

Guillaume's body fell while I was distributing the ammunition, while I was cleaning and reloading rifles. I had no premonition, no pang in my heart when he was shot, no tingle of intuition when he collapsed. Seeing him a few yards away from me, I thought he was out of danger, as if my mere presence would protect him from bullets and wounds, and that he'd be there waiting for me after the battle, that we'd simply take up where we left off.

Guillaume spent six days hovering between life and death. Six days that turned my world upside down. I no longer recognized myself. It was no longer about the suffering of others; it was now my very own. It came out of me with fury, but it also fed on itself quickly, nourished by a secret source that I wasn't controlling. So much came back to me: scenes of my life before the ship ledger, the horror of the crossing, the loss of my mother, the more recent losses—all this suffering was pressing on me, piling up to increase my anguish. I knew that death was a possibility, but I didn't want to lose this little griffe with the big heart when I had just found him. This courageous and generous man who had given me so much in a small amount of time. When Guillaume had spoken to me about the burns that Ma Aza inflicted on her body, I cocked my head in sympathy, but without really understanding. Now I understood how pain can transform us into wild animals with no other recourse than the need to howl at death. I would have preferred being buried alive to feeling the abyss into which I was sinking. Suddenly, I understood Désirée's absent stare, because mine was also being emptied. I felt it in my bones, and they were breaking. Anguish made me stumble, and I would have preferred to never have been born.

When I wasn't at Guillaume's side, I let my body follow the jerky rhythm of my pain and anger, without paying attention to things or people. The desire I felt to punish and seek vengeance, for me and for us, grew uncontrollably and devastatingly in me. My friends didn't dare come close to me, not recognizing the calm and serene Marie Nago in this person with nervous gestures and wild eyes. I avoided Désirée—how could I tell her the news? What do I tell her, then, so that she doesn't collapse?

The fifth day, Master Silo's profile blocked the sun. In a sharp move, the former teacher threw his baton toward me. Instinctively, I reacted with an unusual violence that surprised me. Calmly, Master Silo warded off the blow, dodged it without ever attacking. I charged at him with rage, throwing my baton, turning like a raging animal. A little circle had formed around us. Some were whispering, others were sniggering. I noticed Moussa out of the corner of my eye, watching without saying a word, impassive. I don't know how long this fighting lasted. Besides, was it a fight? Facing me, Master Silo continued to fend off my blows without striking back as I knew he could have done. Sometimes a glimmer of satisfaction, vanishing quickly, would light up his eyes, but he didn't say a word. His movements were always controlled and followed my rhythm. When, exhausted, I finally stopped, Master Silo simply offered me his bottle of *clairin*, a raw white rum made from sugarcane. It's only at that moment that I wiped my tears away.

The beach had been emptied and the sea seemed immense. Silent, I looked at the ocean that connected us to the two worlds: the one that had seen the birth of most of us and the one from which came those who had led us all the way here. An impassive ocean in the face of our victories and our defeats. For ten days now, the ships had taken to the ocean once more, this time bringing only the wounded, the survivors of the war, and the conquered.

We had fought well, but I'd seen so many horrors, seen so much blood flow, lost so much I didn't yet know if I could rejoice. In both camps, death had caused ravages, trampling human life. Slavery had caused so much harm; it had destroyed bodies that had folded up without surrendering, bodies that preferred to mutilate themselves than to bend down, bodies that kept their eyes open even in death. So much blood shed in the name of the wealth that the colony had brought to France and which France didn't want to lose.

These last weeks had been filled with horror and grandeur. These images lingered like a setting sun that didn't want to say good-bye. It was without a doubt the same for many among us. The bloody sounds, the smell of death, but also the numerous acts of courage would remain in the landscape for a long time, as if the battle were continuing endlessly, right under our eyes.

I went to Fort Picolet with the others. I was worn out. All around me, friends were intoxicated with joy, beaming and rowdy. They would lean to hurl insults and jeers at the defeated. Erected in the extreme north of the bay of Au Cap, Picolet made it possible to control and protect the two channels that provided access to Au Cap's harbor. Next to the door made of two large, decorated stands, on the top of the corniche, I saw France's weapons. From the ramparts of Picolet, we could see the sea, the reefs. From there, one could undoubtedly have seen the slave ships that had led the captives to Saint-Domingue. The Atlantic Ocean, far off, would tell our story—my story, Ma Aza's story, and Bashira's story. Today this fort that the French wanted to make "impenetrable" was in the hands of those whom they had called "bandits" and "wild animals." From time to time, a big laugh would burst out, sounding sometimes like a sob. Behind my half-closed eyes, I relived the last moments of the battle, remembering all our efforts to mount the attack on Vertières. The defeats. The dead. The wounded. I could see the horses fall. I could still hear the screams. In order not to see Guillaume's wounded body again and add to this unbearable pain that struck me when I thought of him, I would relive faces seen just for enough time before they disappeared. What had happened to them? Were they wounded or were they dead? I had caught a glimpse of Jérôme Beauvais, the mulatto, who fought with a recklessness that had surprised me a little. Guillaume had told me that Jérôme had enlisted for a while in the French Army before joining us. A young woman with whom I'd had drunk some *clairin* the night before had fallen dead a few steps away from me. In Vertières, I had seen Cécile's brother from the Lespinasse shop where Désirée collected scraps of fabric in the city of Au Cap. How far away all this seemed! So many had disappeared since then! The image of my friend from long ago, Basir, came back to me; I saw Bayi's smiling face and I felt a cold viciousness envelope me. My worry for Guillaume devastated me. It made all the losses even worse, as I wavered under these consecutive disappearances. I no longer wanted to count them, yet it had to be done. We had to honor the dead and care for the living. With Moussa and Master Silo's help, I reviewed the names of friends and acquaintances. To confirm the dead, exchange news of those who were wounded and those who had disappeared. Amédée, Cécile Lespinasse's lover, was very much alive. Her brother Ferdinand was wounded, but his life didn't seem to be in danger. On the other hand, her good friend Angeline Maurepas was dead, as was her military uncle, Pierre Lespinasse. The mulatto, Jérôme Beauvais, had a crushed leg, we didn't yet know whether he was going to pull through. No one knew where Elsa went. We'd been waiting for news of her since Artibonite.

Guillaume survived his wounds. Once again. But this time, death got very close to him. He managed to get away with a weakened body and trembling smile in which I still saw the same serenity as before. I would laugh often and love life, but Guillaume the Griffe—despite his grandfather's abandonment, despite the jeers and insults—held an unwavering faith in humankind. Without a doubt, Aza and Bashira had a lot to do with it. I loved this man who had chosen to fight so that everyone would be treated equally, whether they were black, griffes, or mulattoes. He would need time to recover, but I would be by his side.

I looked around me. It was a late November afternoon, cool and humid. Men and women had gathered, some were a little stunned, others were agitated, not knowing yet what to do with themselves. Someone had put a large saucepan full of water on a wood fire and the smell of ginger and lemon balm soon spread a generous warmth among the group. A flask of clairin was passed from one hand to another. Désirée had settled next to me. At one point, she placed her head on my knees. Over the days, she was becoming less quiet and passive, and we tacitly respected her mood. She'd escape sometimes to be alone, but she also spent a great deal of time with Guillaume, who had finally passed the critical phase of recovery. Her smile mixed in with mine when she would tell us stories that only the little one could invent. I would lift my eyes toward the stars of this November sky that I so loved. The rain had finally stopped, and the stars seemed washed, radiating from a sweet and clear light. There were soldiers lying down on the ground all around, and I began to tell the story of the battle, as if to get closer to Basir, to Zinga the African, to Bayi, to the men and women who had left their lives there. It was also to fill in the silence, to give the wounds time to bleed less. When I began my story, all eyes turned to me. Even those who had fought in it came near. I felt as though my voice no longer belonged to me, it took certain tones that were both intimate and distant, as if I were also addressing those men and women who had departed before seeing this day. Without realizing it, my voice changed like my mother's when she would tell me stories, over there before the ship and its ledger. Also, maybe like Ma Aza's voice when she would tell the children stories that would make their eyes shine.

The friends present added a detail here, some words there; some rose to mime the actions of General Capois. Everyone was talking about him with an admiration that made the most hardened lips tremble. As for the dauntless Moussa, he'd sometimes close his eyes, as if thinking about this man filled him with a feeling he couldn't contain.

Besides me, other people told stories about different feats, citing different names. There were so many, enough to feed our evenings when the need to revisit our disappeared ones made us sullen or angry. Long after telling the stories, we would remain silent. The greatness of all the brave ones was also shared with us, floating around us. I drew from it, with both hands, not only to soothe our suffering but also to wash off all the shameful acts, to face the difficult tomorrows that were waiting for us. Around us, the city was in ruins, and I imagined that this former colony, which had been so wealthy in the past, bore the ravages of war everywhere. My feet, damaged from so many days of walking and being on the lookout, barely carried me, and the loss of so many friends weighed down my steps even more. But I was standing on this land that was finally ours.

To have lost so many friends, to have seen the survivors' distress in front of lifeless bodies, to have seen Guillaume brush so closely to death, enhanced my feeling of belonging to this land. This feeling grew in me when I put my feet on the ground, and my toes sank into the sand, and the wild grass brushed against my calves, and the low-hanging branches of trees brushed against my hair, a timid satisfaction rising up from my legs to my lips. I also saw it in the eyes of the cultivators. Waking up early in the morning, drinking their coffee, savoring a mango, soaking their feet in a stream—every banal and familiar act took on all-new resonance. We were free, all of us were free: African or creoles, blacks, mulattoes, griffes, and all these names that they stuck on us for so long. Are we going to reject them or keep them? Are we going to use them to move forward? Instinctively, I asked myself this question without knowing how to answer it.

The rain had finally stopped. In the distance, I could see the ocean. The silhouette of the departing ships was outlined on the blue waves. Appearing very small from a distance, they carried away the aftermath of the Old World. My memories from before the time of the ledger were now fully a part of me and mixed with my dreams for a more beautiful future. As I watched the ships disappear over the horizon, I was imagining a new world.

AFTERWORD
Annette K. Joseph-Gabriel

The year 1804, Michel-Rolph Trouillot writes, was "a rupture ahead of its time . . . ahead of History as it had been experienced by the world." It was the year Haiti proclaimed its independence from France, having waged a long and bloody revolution to wrest its liberty from the vise grip of the slaveholding empire. Over two centuries later, Haiti's independence continues to resonate as a historical event of monumental meaning, a watershed moment in the making of the Atlantic World. As scholars often remind us, the Haitian Revolution birthed the first free Black republic in the Western Hemisphere. For Michel-Rolph Trouillot, the meaning of this pivotal event reverberates beyond the symbolism and politics of the Atlantic World to interrupt the very idea of history as we know it. As he explains elsewhere, "The Haitian Revolution . . . entered history with the peculiar characteristic of being unthinkable even as it happened" because of "the incapacity of most contemporaries to understand the ongoing revolution on its own terms. They could read the news only with their ready-made categories, and these categories were incompatible with the idea of a slave revolution."[1] In the racist, white supremacist narratives about Black inferiority that underpinned slavery, Black freedom and a sovereign Black republic were impossible to fathom. But the enslaved people on the island of Saint Domingue did in fact successfully attain their freedom from imperial France. "If some events cannot be accepted even as they occur, how can they be assessed later?" Trouillot asks, "How does one write a history of the impossible?"[2]

With *Désirée Congo*, Évelyne Trouillot once again takes up this question about historical narratives which has been a longstanding preoccupation for the Trouillots. Born on January 2,

1954, a day after the 150th anniversary of Haiti's independence, Évelyne has been no stranger to the study and production of Haitian history. Her erudite family counts among its members Évelyne's brothers, Michel-Rolph and Lyonel, an anthropologist and a novelist, respectively, as well as her uncle, Henock, a historian. The Trouillots have left their mark on Haitian history and letters. They have also been for Évelyne an invaluable source of knowledge about those parts of Haitian history that archival documents have not adequately rendered: "the atmosphere of the times, the pulse of society."[3] Évelyne's own publications in French and Kreyòl encompass a range of forms, including novels, short stories, poetry, and theater. Whether it be the sisterhood forged in the terror of the slave ship's hold, or the painful memories of life under the Duvalier dictatorship recounted in *Memory at Bay,* or the grim realities of socioeconomic inequality in contemporary Haiti dramatized in *Le rond-point,* Trouillot's novels always highlight encounters between people who are often thrust together by circumstance and must find a way to live. As Jason Herbeck so compellingly argues, this "dynamic of the encounter" is a hallmark of Trouillot's fine-grained exploration of the very essence of humanity, of our capacity for violence and tenderness, destruction and care.[4] Chronologically, one might consider Trouillot's novel *The Infamous Rosalie,* published nearly two decades prior, as something of a prequel to *Désirée Congo* because the story of love, maternity, and marronage which it tells takes place in the years immediately preceding the Haitian Revolution.

Désirée Congo opens with two epigraphs that outline the stakes of (re)writing history. The first, from Frantz Fanon's *Toward the African Revolution,* is a declaration at once simple and profound: "The plunge into the chasm of the past is the condition and source of freedom." The second, taken from Michel-Rolph's study of Duvalierism as a structural problem that went well beyond the actions of any single dictator, is the above-quoted description of 1804 as an event that overtakes history.[5] Both epigraphs stage a return to the past as a site from which to imagine other futures. They also articulate the possibilities of revolution to bring about not just new political outcomes but new worlds entirely.

Désirée Congo undertakes just such a project of alternative world-making. Set in the uncertainty and turmoil of revolution, in a Saint-Domingue that is on the cusp of becoming something new, the novel explores its protagonists' varied visions of what that new horizon might bring forth. In so doing, Évelyne Trouillot considers the myriad possibilities of freedom's meanings, the sovereign futures that were yet to come, and those that may still yet be. This is a novel that throws into disarray any attempts to plot the certain, linear march of history. Instead, within the pages of *Désirée Congo* we find Fanon's "chasm" and Michel-Rolph's "rupture." And yet, the archival gaps and silences, much lamented elsewhere, here become filled with possibility.

For example, when one of the novel's main characters, Cécile Lespinasse, reflects on stories from the revolutionary battlefield about "women who had fought enemy troops while carrying mattresses to protect themselves from musket fire," she echoes nearly word for word the historian Laurent Dubois's account of "a group of women [who] attacked the French troops while wearing mattresses to protect themselves from musket fire."[6] Who were these women? What war cry did they shout or what freedom song did they sing as they charged into battle? Did they see themselves as sisters-in-arms or as strangers thrust together for a time by a common enemy? Likely because the archival sources say, "There is nothing here. This is an unthinkable story," the historical account offers no more information about the mattress-wielding women. As Évelyne Trouillot explains, "The historian cannot always afford the luxury of dwelling on these elements, but the novelist must without fail concern herself with them in order to give her characters depth."[7] Trouillot does more than provide alternative details about women in the Haitian Revolution born from a fiction writer's imagination. By crafting a world in which women taking up arms for their freedom in the eighteenth century is neither a novelty nor an exception, her representation of women in combat deepens our understanding of revolutionary Saint-Domingue as it in fact was, a world that nevertheless remained unthinkable and unspeakable for many of those who authored the narratives that today constitute the archive.

Throughout *Désirée Congo,* Trouillot shows the way toward how one might tell an impossible story by crafting a polyphonic narrative that allows the disruptive and world-building power of language to shine through. Each of the novel's chapters is narrated from the perspective of one of its seven major characters: Zinga, a relative newcomer who arrives in Saint-Domingue as a captive aboard one of the last ships to ply the slave trade; Aza, who finds pleasure, comradeship, and sisterhood in the arms of another enslaved woman; Désirée Congo, Aza's love child who survived the Middle Passage in her mother's womb and is birthed in a land of horror and beauty; Guillaume, the mixed-race boy mothered by Aza; Marie Nago, the grim, tenacious maroon who takes up arms during the revolution and who eventually learns to laugh again; Jérôme Beauvais, the son of an enslaved woman and a white planter who must find his place in a society in turmoil; and Cécile Lespinasse, the somewhat sheltered daughter of a wealthy Black family whose journal becomes a site of expression for her revolutionary ideals. By giving voice to this chorus of characters, Trouillot presents a nuanced picture of the lives of Saint-Domingue's inhabitants that exceeds the usual dichotomies of black and white, enslaver and enslaved. The entangled lives and testimonies of characters who sometimes find that there is far more that binds them than divides them give rise to a composite narrative that, in telling the story of the Haitian Revolution "from below," shifts the focus from military strategy and political maneuvering to the stuff of everyday living. Ultimately, these varied but intertwined stories attest to survival and the possibility of making a life even amid terror and uncertainty.

But not all testimonies are created equal, the novel seems to suggest. As the only characters who narrate their stories in the first person (all others are narrated in the third person), Désirée Congo and Marie Nago function as doubles for each other. The two are polar opposites in many ways. Marie Nago's determination not only to survive but to make a life for herself quite literally roots her in Saint-Domingue: "I had accepted my life on this island, in these mountains that had become a part of me, as if some of this red, humid earth had taken root under my skin, permeating it with its smells and its mystery. I had chosen to live and to live here." The island that implants itself under Marie Nago's skin is something altogether different from the one that inhabits another enslaved woman's body in *The Infamous Rosalie*. There, in that more somber, brutal Saint-Domingue, the enslaved Marie-Pierre "seems an extension of the earth itself, with her small body, and her skin, a cracked reddish mountain hue. She smells of sugarcane since she spends her whole life pushing cane stalks through the rollers."[8] Here, in *Désirée Congo*, Trouillot imagines Marie Nago's body as more than commodity and repository of violence. Hers is a body that becomes one with an island that—while no less brutal—is also, ultimately, home.

In contrast, Désirée Congo does not take root on the island but rather seems to take flight, retreating into the world of her own mind which is populated by the dead children whose young lives in slavery were cut short by harrowing violence. Unlike Marie Nago, who is as tangible as the baton she learns to wield with deadly efficiency in battles against the French Army, Désirée Congo is a haunting presence who hovers at the edges of spaces. She flits through the narrative wraithlike, carrying within her the torment and companionship of the children whose voices only she can hear. The multicolored fabrics that Désirée trails in her wake become like Ariadne's thread, guiding us through the convulsions of that painful transition from bondage to freedom, and through the attendant stories of survival that are filled with pain and loss. Despite their differences, both Marie Nago and Désirée Congo share the ability to speak the "I," a self-articulation that allows them to put words to the immense grief of the losses they suffer and witness. They share too their composite names made up of a moniker acquired in slavery and a geographic location that is more ghostly memory than homeland. By their names, Désirée Congo and Marie Nago straddle two worlds, much like the Caribbean drummers and dancers of Suzanne Césaire's *The Great Camouflage,* for whom "Antilles-Africa . . . the nostalgia for earthly spaces lives on in the[ir] hearts."⁹ The Haiti that emerges in this novel is not a space of negation and erasure, defined solely by the displacement, deracination, and fracture wrought by slavery. It is also a place that continent-straddling women can call home.

Désirée Congo occupies a somewhat unique place in the literary history of important works about the Haitian Revolution because much like *The Infamous Rosalie,* it is first and foremost a story about everyday life, about ordinary people living through extraordinary times. Trouillot explains the reason for her choice, in both novels, of characters who have otherwise faded into obscurity: ". . . my characters' anonymity allowed me to portray real individuals with complex personalities, escaping what expectations the reader might have for extant historical figures."¹⁰ In Trouillot's novels, we do not find the representation of the rise and fall of revolutionary heroes that we find in Aimé Césaire's *Et les chiens se taisaient (And the Dogs Were Silent)* and *The Tragedy of King Christophe* or Édouard Glissant's *Monsieur Toussaint.* It is neither "lo real maravilloso" of Alejo Carpentier's *The Kingdom of This World,* nor the sweeping history of an undifferentiated mass of slaves rising up against their masters in C. L. R. James's *The Black Jacobins.*¹¹ *Désirée Congo* is, at its core, a story about people. It foregrounds love and family and intimacy, not as de facto acts of resistance, but as the very essence of being human. Trouillot accomplishes this by displacing the Haitian Revolution from the fore of the narrative and relegating it to a muted rumbling in the background. Throughout the story, the characters are only aware of snatches of information about the actions and motivations of political leaders, and they struggle to make sense of what is happening and what it all means. Trouillot shows that the collection of events that we have come to unify under the umbrella term the Haitian Revolution was, in its contemporaneous moment, a time of turmoil whose outcome was obscure and far from certain for those who lived through it.

With this novel, Évelyne Trouillot does more than offer possibilities for telling an impossible story. She also gives us language to articulate an answer to the related question, why tell this story in the first place? In the wake of the decisive Battle of

Vertières that led to the defeat and withdrawal of Napoleon's troops from the island—a battle that Trouillot explains elsewhere has been erased from Western history—Marie Nago says that she looked around at her battle-weary compatriots and began to tell a story:[12]

> I began to tell the story of the battle, as if to get closer to Basir, to Zinga the African, to Bayi, to the men and women who had left their lives there. It was also to fill in the silence, to give the wounds time to bleed less. When I began to tell my story, all eyes turned to me. Even those who had fought in it came near. I felt as though my voice no longer belonged to me, it took certain tones that were both intimate and distant, as if I were also addressing those men and women who had departed before seeing this day. Without realizing it, my voice changed like my mother's when she would tell me stories, over there before the ship and its ledger. Also, maybe like Ma Aza's voice when she would tell the children stories that would make their eyes shine.

Were its purpose to serve as yet another recounting of the history of the Haitian Revolution, those familiar with this history might find *Désirée Congo* to be somewhat superfluous. But, as Marie Nago explains, even those who had fought in the battle and knew the events intimately drew near to hear her speak of it. Storytelling has transformative power. It molds Marie Nago's voice such that she can speak of, for, and as the mothers whose maternity we are told slavery nullified and rendered impossible. As Marie Nago's story unfolds, her comrades add their own details in an act of collective naming and narration. If French history will not tell of the losses and triumphs of the Battle of Vertières, here, in the pages of a novel, a maroon will clear a space for the voices that were never silent, only unacknowledged. This is what it means "to honor the dead and care for the living." This is what it means to stand in the past and survey uncertain futures, some already closed off by the tenacious legacy of slavery, others full of the promise that other worlds are possible. As Anne McClintock so succinctly expressed,

"History is a series of social fabulations that we cannot do without. It is an inventive practice, but not just any invention will do. For it is the future, not the past, that is at stake in the contest over which memories survive."[13] What would it mean if we privileged the memories of the fictional Marie Nago over the chasms and ruptures of history? "My memories from before the time of the ledger were now fully a part of me and mixed with my dreams for a more beautiful future. As I watched the ships disappear over the horizon, I was imagining a new world." With its keen focus on the interior lives of African and Creole characters caught in a turbulent revolution but determined not to be swept away by it, *Désirée Congo* offers us a nuanced view of the past. But it is, above all, a story about the future.

Notes

1. Michel-Rolph Trouillot, *Silencing the Past: Power and the Production of History* (Boston: Beacon Press, 1995), 72.
2. Ibid.
3. Évelyne Trouillot, "Le roman historique: Une quête de sens du présent," *Revue d'histoire Haïtienne* 1 (2019): 547. Translations mine.
4. Jason Herbeck, review of *Le rond-point*, by Évelyne Trouillot, *Journal of Haitian Studies* 22, no. 1 (Spring 2016): 190.
5. Michel-Rolph Trouillot, *Les racines historiques de l'État duvaliérien* (Port-au-Prince: Éditions Deschamps, 1986).
6. Laurent Dubois, *Haiti: The Aftershocks of History* (New York: Metropolitan Books, 2012), 38.
7. É. Trouillot, "Le roman historique," 546.
8. Évelyne Trouillot, *The Infamous Rosalie*, trans. Marjorie Salvodon (Lincoln: University of Nebraska Press, 2013), 87.
9. Suzanne Césaire, "The Great Camouflage," in *The Great Camouflage: Writings of Dissent (1941–1945)*, ed. Daniel Maximin, trans. Keith Walker (Middletown, CT.: Wesleyan University Press, 2012), 45.
10. É. Trouillot, "Le roman historique," 543.
11. Aimé Césaire, *Et les chiens se taisaient: Tragédie: Arrangement théâtral* (Paris: Présence Africaine, 1956); Aimé Césaire, *The*

Tragedy of King Christophe: A Play (New York: Grove Press, 1969); Édouard Glissant, *Monsieur Toussaint* (Washington D.C.: Three Continents Press, 1981); Alejo Carpentier, *The Kingdom of This World,* trans. Harriet De Onis (New York: Farrar, Straus & Giroux, 2006); C. L. R. James, *The Black Jacobins: Toussaint L'Ouverture and the San Domingo Revolution,* 2nd ed. (New York: Random House, 1963).

12. Évelyne Trouillot, "Haïti nous permet de mieux comprendre l'humanité," *Haïtii Inter,* 1 April 2023, https://www.youtube.com/watch?v=_lGvA4sok1U.

13. Anne McClintock, *Imperial Leather: Race, Gender, and Sexuality in the Colonial Contest* (New York: Routledge, 1995), 328.

BIBLIOGRAPHY

Clerfeuille, L. "Marronnage au feminin dans Rosalie L'infâme d'Évelyne Trouillot." *Contemporary French and Francophone Studies* 16, no. 1 (2012): 33–44.
Danticat, Edwidge, and Évelyne Trouillot. "Evelyne Trouillot." *Bomb* (2004): 48–53.
Dash, J. M., Dany Laferrière, Louis-Philippe Dalembert, Edwidge Danticat, and Évelyne Trouillot. "Roundtable: Writing, History, and Revolution." *Small Axe* 9, no. 2 (2005): 189–99.
Dupuy, Alex, Robert Fatton, Évelyne Trouillot, and Tatiana Wah. "Twenty-First-Century Haiti—A New Normal? A Conversation with Four Scholars of Haiti." In *The Idea of Haiti: Rethinking Crisis and Development*, edited by Millery Polyné, 243–68. Minneapolis: University of Minnesota Press, 2013.
Herbeck, Jason. "Entretien avec Évelyne Trouillot." *French Review* 82, no. 4 (2009): 822.
Jean-Charles, Régine Michelle. *Looking for Other Worlds: Black Feminism and Haitian Fiction*. Charlottesville: University of Virginia Press, 2022.
Jonassaint, Jean. "For the Trouillots: An Afterword to the English Translation of *Ti Difé Boulé Sou Istoua Ayiti*." In *Stirring the Pot of Haitian History*, by Michel-Rolph Trouillot, edited by Mariana F. Past and Benjamin Hebblethwaite. Liverpool: Liverpool University Press, 2021.
Joseph-Gabriel, Annette. "'Tant de silence à briser': Entretien avec Évelyne Trouillot." *Nouvelles Études Francophones* 32, no. 1 (2017): 82–94.
Larrier, R. "In[her]itance: Legacies and Lifelines in Évelyne Trouillot's *Rosalie L'infâme*." *Dalhousie French Studies* 88 (2009): 135–46.
Mehta, Brinda J. *Notions of Identity, Diaspora, and Gender in Caribbean Women's Writing*. New York: Palgrave Macmillan, 2009.
Munro, Martin, ed. *Haiti Rising: Haitian History, Culture and the Earthquake of 2010*. Liverpool: Liverpool University Press, 2010.
Palimpsest: A Journal on Women, Gender, and the Black International, vol. 8, no.1 (2019). Special issue on Évelyne Trouillot.
Trouillot, Évelyne. *Absences sans frontières*. Montpellier: Chèvre Feuille Étoilée, 2013.
———. "Besoins primaires." *Haïti parmi les vivants*. Arles: Actes Sud, 2010.

———. "Eternity Lasted Less than Sixty Seconds." *Haitian History: New Perspectives* (2012): 312–16.

———. *Je m'appelle Fridhomme*. Delmas: C3 Éditions, 2017.

———. *La chambre interdite: Nouvelles*. Paris: L'Harmattan, 1996.

———. "Lakay Se Lakay, but Where Is Lakay? Home Is Home but Where Is Home?" *Cultural Dynamics* 30 (2018): 13–18.

———. *La mémoire aux abois*. Paris: Hoëbeke, 2010. Translated by Paul Curtis Daw as *Memory at Bay* (Charlottesville: University of Virginia Press, 2015).

———. *Le bleu de l'île (The Blue of the Island). Journal of Haitian Studies* 18, no. 2 (2012): 210–64.

———. *Le mirador aux étoiles*. Port-au-Prince: L'Imprimeur II, 2007.

———. *L'Œil-totem*. Port-au-Prince: Presses Nationales d'Haïti, 2006.

———. *Le rond-point*. Port-au-Prince: L'Imprimeur, 2015.

———. *Parlez-moi d'amour*. Port-au-Prince: Bibliothèque nationale d'Haïti, 2002.

———. "Primal Needs." Translated by Paul Curtis Daw. *Words without Borders: The Online Magazine for International Literature,* January 2013. Accessed March 19, 2024. https://www.wordswithoutborders.org/article/bilingual/primal-needs.

———. *Rosalie l'infâme*. Paris: Dapper, 2003. Translated by Marjorie Salvodon as *The Infamous Rosalie* (Lincoln: University of Nebraska Press, 2013).

Ulysse, Gina A. *Why Haiti Needs New Narratives: A Post-Quake Chronicle*. Middletown, CT: Wesleyan University Press, 2015.

Recent books in the series
CARAF Books
Caribbean and African Literature
Translated from French

The Last of the African Kings
Maryse Condé, translated by Richard Philcox

Popa Singer
René Depestre, translated by Kaiama L. Glover

Crusoe's Footprint
Patrick Chamoiseau, translated by Charly Verstraet and Jeffrey Landon Allen

I Am Alive
Kettly Mars, translated by Nathan H. Dize

Wandering Memory
Jan J. Dominique, translated by Emma Donovan Page

Humus
Fabienne Kanor, translated by Lynn E. Palermo

The Belle Créole
Maryse Condé, translated by Nicole Simek

Dézafi
Frankétienne, translated by Asselin Charles

Do You Hear in the Mountains . . . and Other Stories
Maïssa Bey, translated by Erin Lamm

I Die by This Country
Fawzia Zouari, translated by Skyler Artes

The Leopard Boy
Daniel Picouly, translated by Jeanne Garane

Memory at Bay
Évelyne Trouillot, translated by Paul Curtis Daw

Arabic as a Secret Song
Leïla Sebbar, translated by Skyler Artes

The Other Side of the Sea
Louis-Philippe Dalembert, translated by Robert H. McCormick Jr.

The Fury and Cries of Women
Angèle Rawiri, translated by Sara Hanaburgh

Far from My Father
Véronique Tadjo, translated by Amy Baram Reid

Climb to the Sky
Suzanne Dracius, translated by Jamie Davis

Land and Blood
Mouloud Feraoun, translated by Patricia Geesey

"At the Café" and "The Talisman"
Mohammed Dib, translated by C. Dickson

The Little Peul
Mariama Barry, translated by Carrol F. Coates

Aunt Résia and the Spirits and Other Stories
Yanick Lahens, translated by Betty Wilson

Above All, Don't Look Back
Maïssa Bey, translated by Senja L. Djelouah

A Rain of Words: A Bilingual Anthology of Women's Poetry in Francophone Africa
Irène Assiba d'Almeida, editor, translated by Janis A. Mayes

The Abandoned Baobab: The Autobiography of a Senegalese Woman
Ken Bugul, translated by Marjolijn de Jager

Dog Days: An Animal Chronicle
Patrice Nganang, translated by Amy Baram Reid

The Land without Shadows
Abdourahman A. Waberi, translated by Jeanne Garane

The Poor Man's Son: Menrad, Kabyle Schoolteacher
Mouloud Feraoun, translated by Lucy R. McNair

Exile according to Julia
Gisèle Pineau, translated by Betty Wilson